"What we shared
obsession, nothing m
less, and it was the
in hell." ~ Rafe

TORRENT

CONDEMNED SERIES: BOOK ONE

GEMMA JAMES

Gemma James

TORRENT

Edited by Jessica Nollkamper
Cover designed by Gemma James
Cover image used under license from www.bigstockphoto.com

ISBN-13: 978-1499589115
ISBN-10: 1499589115

NOTE TO READERS

TORRENT is a new adult dark romance with disturbing themes and explicit content, including sexual scenes and violence that may offend some. Intended for mature audiences. Part one of the CONDEMNED series. This is not a stand-alone read. Approximately 43,000 words.

TITLES BY GEMMA JAMES
(a pseudonym for Christina Jean Michaels)

Titles written as Gemma James:
ULTIMATUM (The Devil's Kiss #1)
ENSLAVED (The Devil's Kiss #2)
RETRIBUTION (The Devil's Kiss #3)
THE DEVIL'S KISS TRILOGY (The Devil's Kiss #1-3)
THE DEVIL'S SALVATION: FINAL EPILOGUE (The Devil's Kiss #4)
THE DEVIL'S KISS: COMPLETE SERIES
TORRENT (Condemned #1)
RAMPANT (Condemned #2 - coming October 2014)

Titles written as Christina Jean Michaels:
EPIPHANY (Legacy of Payne #1)
AWAKENING (Legacy of Payne #2 – coming late 2014)
UNHINGED (Legacy of Payne #3 – release date undetermined)

To my husband James, whose support and encouragement means everything to me. Thanks for believing in me, even when I didn't believe in myself. I love you.

PROLOGUE

ALEX

We'd left the gravesite two hours ago, but Mom's lifeless eyes still accused me. The memory of finding her dead in the bathtub, the water deep and murky with her blood, embedded in my brain like a tattoo I couldn't erase.

I stood in my bedroom, a space inundated with white lacy subterfuge, and sensed the uprising in my soul. Grief turned and boiled with a vengeance. I clenched my hands and crossed them over heaving breasts but couldn't stop the eruption. I'd been simmering too long, unchecked. I hated my perfect room, my perfect family, my perfect life. Appearances were deceitful bitches that lied and covered the ugly truth.

"Open the door, Lex!" Frantic fists pounded, and I covered my ears to block out my step-brother's barrage on the door. The first drop of misery fell from my eyes and despite squeezing them shut, I was incapable of stemming the mental pictures. They flickered in my head like a child's View-Master reel.

I relived Mom's horrified expression the night she heard me cry out, recalled the condemnation in her voice when she yelled at Zach to get out of my room. I still saw her wide eyes—the same green as mine—staring at me blankly a few days later, open and void as the life bled from her wrists.

"Let me in!"

"Go away!" I screamed, repulsed by the mere sound of his voice. A sob caught in my throat, and my body shook with the effort of holding back. I was trapped inside myself, a prisoner of rage and despair. Bursting with the need to tear into something, I dug my nails into my arms.

Her face wouldn't leave my mind. Her beautiful face, twisted with shock and disgust at what she'd walked in on. I'd been too ashamed to explain. Now it was too late. I'd never see her again, never again inhale the sweet scent of jasmine as she embraced me.

Zach's fault. *My* fault.

My nails dragged down pale flesh, almost of their own volition, and left behind ugly red streaks. Letting out a roar, I hefted a chair into the vanity mirror. My reflection shattered with an echo, a grotesque replica of my soul. I was unstoppable, insane with the need to destroy, to create the sound over and over again. Breaths coming in shallow gasps, I swept candles onto the floor, followed by pictures and perfumes. My entire makeup collection crashed onto the white carpet where the colors stained with flawless imperfection, but the pressure in my chest wouldn't subside.

The assault on my door grew in strength, and I thought I picked up another voice blending with Zach's. Had to be my imagination. Dad had barricaded himself in his bedroom, just like me, though he had a sedative and a bottle of Jack to keep him company.

Afternoon sunshine streamed through the lace curtains, an assault of warmth on my face, and I scowled. The skies should have opened, should have drenched the earth until it drowned. On that day, the day I'd watched my mother go into the ground, the whole fucking world should've cried until their eyes bled.

I grasped the lamp on my nightstand and hurtled it through the window, eliciting that glorious sound of splintering glass again, and I screamed until my voice went raw like the rest of me. The door broke under Zach's struggle to get inside, and I fell backward, landing hard on the bed with both hands raised.

"Leave me alone," I said with a pleading sob. He'd

never gone so far as to break down my door. My room had been my only sanctuary, other than those few horrible occasions when I found him lying in wait in the darkness; those times when I wasn't quick enough to escape within my four walls and turn the lock. "Don't touch me!"

Strong hands encircled my wrists and pulled them to the sides, but it was Rafe's beautiful green eyes staring back and not my brother's. Tension seeped from my bones, left me weightless, and I exhaled in relief when he knelt in front of me, elbows resting on my thighs. A significant moment passed, locking the two of us in that short span of time when the world magically receded.

"I've got you. Everything's gonna be okay." His arms wound around my trembling body, and I went limp in the cocoon of his embrace.

Zach stood off to the side, arms crossed and gaze shooting daggers in our direction. I stiffened under the threat of his jealousy, and not even Rafe's warmth could combat the chill that seized me. I wanted to believe him so badly, but nothing would ever be okay again.

1. ESCAPE

ALEX

Eight Years Later

When it came to karma, I wished for skepticism. Thing was, I fully believed in karma. Something had to balance the scales, otherwise the world would tip off its axis and crash into total chaos. Thanks to my belief in supernatural balance, I had no doubt I was screwed. That was never more true than when I gripped the single piece of paper on which four words were written.

I'm coming for you.

I'd found the note tacked to my door. I didn't question who left it, as only one person had reason to leave such a warning, and considering he'd been released from the state penitentiary three weeks ago, I couldn't deny the evidence. I'd been agonizing over the moment when he would confront me.

When, not if.

My knees gave out, and I sank to the bed. Rain beat against the roof in a sudden onslaught, and the panes of my favorite window seat rattled. I hadn't been home for more than a few minutes, but apparently I'd escaped inside at the most opportune time. I took the torrential tap-tap-tap and rush of wind as a sign, an omen perhaps.

He was coming for me, and I deserved it.

Someone pounded on the door, and I jumped like a frightened kitten. I stashed the note in the drawer of my nightstand and returned to the foyer, pulled the door open, and almost expected to find Rafe on the other side.

It was Zach, not Rafe, who shoved past the threshold. Immediately, the strong odor of whiskey hit my nose.

"You're not fuckin' marrying him," he said with a slur. I edged away as he stumbled into the accent table in the foyer. "I'm going crazy, Lex. Look what you've done to me." Wiping soggy brown hair from his eyes, he lurched forward and clung to my shoulder to keep from falling.

"Did you drive here?"

"Of course I didn't drive! I'm not an idiot."

"I know you're not an—"

He grabbed my chin, silencing me instantly. "You're gonna call this engagement off, do you hear me?"

The ever-present weight of dread held me in its clutches. “Dad pushed for it.” I paused, one, two, three thuds of my heart pounding in my ears. “Just like he pushed for me to date Lucas. I think he knows.”

“Knows what?” His fingers fell from my chin, and I stared at my feet, enclosed in trendy black heels that matched the black cocktail dress I’d worn to dinner, where Lucas Perrone had proposed.

“About us.”

He faltered, mouth gaping, and it was the most unusual sight. Zach didn’t normally struggle for words, threats, insults.

He blinked and the moment was gone. “I don’t give a fuck what Dad knows or doesn’t know. You’re gonna break this engagement, and you’re not seeing him again.” As if the issue were settled, he staggered into the living room where he sprawled onto the sofa, one leg bent and a foot resting on the floor. I averted my gaze from the bulge behind his zipper.

I needed to get him out of my house pronto. “I’ll call you a cab. We’ll talk tomorrow about this, I promise.”

He let out a bitter laugh. “My cab just left, and we’re talkin’ now.” His brows narrowed over angry hazel eyes. “C’mere,” he said, patting his lap.

I backed up, shaking my head.

“No? You want it extra rough? Is that it?”

I didn’t want it at all, but I knew better than to voice

it. I scratched my arm, digging in a little deeper than usual.

"You think marrying some mid-forties vanilla hack is gonna 'fix' you? Make you normal? We both know you're nothing but a slut."

I clenched my teeth. His insult maimed more than his hands did, especially since he was the only man I'd ever slept with. He perceived any guy who glanced in my direction as a threat, as if I welcomed the attention, and he'd become downright vicious since Dad set me up with Lucas.

Dad had always made decisions for me, from what school I attended to which program I chose as a major. I'd earned degrees in accounting and business but harbored no desire to use them. He expected me to hop on board the family legacy in a managerial capacity, but unlike him and Zach, I had no interest in mixed martial arts or running an enterprise of venues and training centers.

I chalked it up to the fact that we didn't share DNA. Mom married Abott De Luca when I was six, but he *was* like a dad to me, especially since he'd legally adopted me, and as such, I'd never thought of Zach as a step-brother. Not where it counted. The step part got lost in the sea of right and wrong and perversely unacceptable.

I folded my arms and put another foot of distance between us, backing toward the foyer. No one made me more uncomfortable in my own house, in my own skin, than my own brother.

He seemed pissed that I wasn't rising to his bait by responding. "You're my slut, aren't you, Lex?" He pushed off the couch, as if he only now realized I was retreating, and gripped my arms. "My little whore who loves to be fucked."

"You're hurting me," I said, barely above a whisper, but his fingers pressed harder when I tried to pull away.

"Not as much as you're hurting me!" He drove forward and slammed me into the wall, trapping both wrists on either side of my face. "You know we belong together. You'll never keep me away. *Never.*"

"Let me go."

He brought his face close, lip slightly curled, and his hazel eyes stalled on the ring adorning my left hand. I unfurled my fist until the large diamond scraped the wall, hidden from his line of view. "I won't stand by and watch you marry that bastard. I'll kill myself, just like your mom."

I gasped as the familiar, crushing reminder of Mom ate away at what was left of me. I had no words for him, no protests or pleas. He tossed out the threat to hurt me, like he always did. I wondered if he'd go through with it this time. I tried to imagine him gone, but instead of despair, I found the remnants of sorrow and the promise of relief. Shame accompanied both, as I shouldn't feel sorrow after the things he'd done, and I shouldn't feel relief because he was still my brother.

"Say something!" He cried, shaking me, his face a contortion of bewilderment. "Didn't you hear me? I'm not kidding! I'll do it."

"You don't know what you're saying. You've been drinking—"

"I know exactly what I'm saying. I don't wanna live if I can't have you. Say you won't marry him."

"I won't marry him." I swallowed hard and counted the seconds. Five in, hold, five out. Repeat. All the while, I prayed he'd let the issue drop, let me go and walk out the door.

He had other things in mind. His mouth smashed against mine, tongue forcing my lips apart and plundering. I didn't fight him. I'd learned long ago it didn't do any good. He'd only get rougher, meaner, and in turn, my fucked up body would only get off easier.

I kept my eyes shut and wished to be somewhere else. Anywhere else. The distinctive slide of his zipper rang loudly in my ears, and his hands blazed where he cupped my ass and lifted.

"That's my girl," he breathed as I automatically wound my legs around him, dress bunching at my waist. He pulled my panties to the side and pushed in with a grunt. His fingers banded around my wrists, pinned them to the wall above my head, and he pounded into me, shoving me higher with each forceful thrust. I held back the vomit burning in my throat.

One more thrust, another grunt. "No more Lucas," he said.

"No more Lucas." My face tightened as his tempo increased.

"No more avoiding me."

I agreed to that too. I agreed to anything he wanted when he fucked me. The alternative always left me battered, bruised, and torn to pieces emotionally because the more I fought him, the more he set out to hurt me beyond what I could handle, and that usually meant he brought up Rafe and what he could do to him if I didn't comply.

That threat carried more weight than ever.

Zach didn't last long, probably because it'd been a couple of weeks since he'd last cornered me alone. Lucas' presence had gone a long way in offering some form of protection, but I wasn't so naive as to think he could act as a barrier forever. Even marrying him wouldn't do that.

Zach finally loosened his grasp and allowed my feet to touch the floor. I rubbed my arms where the red impressions from his fingers marred my skin, making the faint, white scars from my nails more noticeable. He took my face in his hands, fingers gouging my jaw, and his gaze bored into me, through me.

"You didn't get off."

"I did," I said quickly, because not reaching orgasm always angered him. "I swear I—"

"You *didn't* get off. Don't try to fake it. I'll always know." Stepping back, he gestured toward my dress. "Take it off."

"C'mon, Zach, you don't have—"

"*Take* it off."

I unzipped the dress and let it fall to my feet, and my breasts jiggled in their braless state. He shoved me across the room, down to the couch, and forced my thighs open. Sinking to his knees, he yanked me toward his mouth until my ass was half off the couch, my legs dangling on either side of his shoulders.

The instant he tore my panties from my body, my mind went blank, as the sounds of my cries were too degrading to acknowledge. I vaguely recalled him twisting my nipples in unforgiving pinches, then slapping my breasts hard. He jammed his fingers into my pussy mercilessly, and after he'd compelled an orgasm from me, he made me suck my own cum off, shoving his fingers deep into my mouth as he emphasized how *he* was the one who had made me come.

Only me, Lex. No one else.

Then he was gone, and I was in the scalding shower, eyes squeezed shut, fists crossed over tender breasts to keep from bloodying my knuckles on the tile. The only drops of water on my cheeks came from the shower head. I never cried. I didn't allow myself the luxury. My breaths came out in soft shudders, and I tried to keep myself in one piece as I recalled what he'd asked before he left.

Do you still love him?

My denial hadn't placated him, and his parting words blared through my head, more forceful than my shame. *If you go anywhere near him, I'll fuck him up for life. He's a lot easier to get to now, isn't he?*

The thought of my brother hurting Rafe terrified me, so I'd told Zach I hadn't heard from him. A lie, because I was pretty sure the note came from Rafe.

Was this always going to be my life? Lies upon lies, sprinkled with the occasional half-truth?

I could leave. I'd considered it before, had even tried once, though I only made it halfway to the California border before chickening out. Too many people close to me had suffered, like the guy I'd teamed up with my Junior year for a science project. He made the mistake of hitting on me, and Zach had given him the nastiest beat down of his life, leaving broken bones and bloody flesh in his wake. Dad's money swept that one under the rug.

There had been others, some no one knew about because Zach was intimidating enough without his reputation as a fighter to keep most quiet. They suffered his rage in silence. Fear of retaliation wasn't the only thing keeping me from fleeing though. I'd hung on to the stupid, absurd, *fanciful* hope that Rafe would someday forgive me.

Impossible. What I'd done was unforgivable.

Standing at a crossroads of sorts, I needed to find the strength to move on with my life. I glanced at the enormous engagement ring Lucas had pushed onto my finger earlier that night. No matter what Dad believed, tying myself to a man I didn't love wouldn't fix anything. Neither would continuing to allow Zach free rein of my puppet strings.

For the first time in your life, Alexandra, do the right thing.

The voice sounded like my father's. Certainly, the words were something he'd say, something he'd said again and again every time I fucked up. And I fucked up a lot. My whole life was one big fuck up.

I shut off the water, wrapped a towel around my body, and entered the bedroom, then changed into jeans and a sweatshirt before pulling a duffle from the closet. I blindly flung clothes onto the bed and stuffed some into the bag. The stash of cash I'd saved, tucked underneath the mattress, also went inside. Lastly, I tossed in my wallet. I didn't need anything else. Just myself and the courage to leave.

That was the hard part.

I took off the ring and let it drop onto the nightstand, then I closed my eyes and envisioned my escape. I'd walk down the hall, feet sinking into the plush runner one last time. I saw myself crack the door open and peek outside, saw myself hop down the stairs of the porch, my paranoid gaze buzzing around as I approached the Volvo Dad had given me for graduation.

The alluring taste of freedom, only a few feet away, tempted with promise. I just had to close the distance and take the first step. I left the bedroom and moved toward the foyer, like a teenager sneaking out past curfew. I felt like a child, excitement fluttering in my belly as my hand neared the doorknob.

Trepidation also stirred in my gut. If I disappeared, would Zach really hurt Rafe, a man he'd once called his best friend?

A knock sounded, and I jerked my fingers back. A few tense seconds passed before the knock repeated. For someone terrified of escaping the shackles of a life unwanted, I should have given more thought to the possibilities on the other side of that door. Swinging the duffle to my back, I pulled it open, and my breath whooshed from me as I uttered his name.

"Rafe."

He was here, standing in front of me, and my knees almost buckled, weaker now than when I'd first spied his note upon returning home. A violent blast of air and rain blew in with his presence, carrying a hint of roses from the bushes off the porch. The aroma infused me with a sense of serenity despite the darkness shadowing my street.

I was the perfect prey in that moment, too stunned to keep my head. I stumbled back, a mistake on my part because he was the second man that night to shove his way into my house.

2. COMEUPPANCE

RAFE

I'd always fantasized about taking a woman, *really* taking a woman, and until Alex had destroyed me with a single lie, the fantasy had only been the depraved thoughts of a man who still had his moral compass intact. A lot could change in eight years. Fuck, I remembered her as the 15-year-old girl she'd been, so I had trouble thinking of Alex as a woman. My dick didn't have the same problem; it couldn't wait to get her alone on Mason Island.

Engaging the deadbolt, I leaned against the door and stared at her with a nonchalance I didn't feel. God help me, but I couldn't take my eyes off all those dark curls cascading over her tiny shoulders. The slender slope of her neck drew my attention, and I imagined closing my hands around her throat and squeezing the essence from her, imagined the panic in her eyes as she neared loss of consciousness.

"Miss me?" I asked.

Her eyes, already wide at the sight of me, grew even rounder. "What?"

I crossed my arms, aware of how my biceps bulged. "I didn't stutter, sweetheart. It's been a long time. Did you miss me?"

"Did I…?" She shook her head, as if I'd uttered the most ridiculous question she'd ever heard. "What do you want, Rafe?" Her words fell from her lips in a nervous whisper.

"I think you already know." You couldn't send an innocent man to prison without expecting some sort of consequences. Except Alex didn't know two fucks about me. The real Rafe Mason was about to do reprehensible things to her, like toss her deceitful naked ass into a cage.

Her gaze veered to the floor, and I barked at her to look at me.

"If I could change things, I would," she said, inching back, a fist rising to her mouth to hide her trembling lips.

"Would you now?" I tilted my head. "What would you do differently? Would you take it back, what, a week later? A month? Maybe after I'd been in there a couple of years? *Eight fucking years*, Alex. That's what you took from me."

"I don't know what you want from me." Two more steps back.

I pushed away from the door and followed, hand sliding into my coat pocket to finger the syringe. "I want to know why you lied." I'd waited so long to ask that question, and the set of her jaw told me she wasn't going to answer. "You didn't even have the guts to face me at the trial." She'd refused to make eye contact, even once. That hadn't surprised me nearly as much as Zach's cold shoulder treatment. How he believed I'd do something so vile, to Alex of all people, was beyond comprehension. She must have put on quite the performance for her family, because her testimony in court had been mechanical, as if she'd read from a script.

She'd stripped everything from me in that courtroom. My career, friends, freedom, and she'd displayed no emotion while doing it.

"I-I can't do this now," she said, a tremor stringing her words together. "I have to go." Darting past me, she made a run for the door and managed to fling it open by the time I whirled around. That's when the duffle swinging on her shoulder caught my attention, and it dawned on me she was running.

Because of the note I'd left on her door? Guess my mind-fuckery had done the trick, only I never expected her to take off. There was no way she could know what I had planned for her. Before she escaped the house, I shot an arm out and slammed the door shut, then pressed into her soft curves that fit perfectly against me.

"You're not going anywhere." Even in that heady moment, as adrenaline pumped through my veins, I hesitated. What I was about to do changed everything. I was about to become the criminal they'd accused me of being.

But no one deserved comeuppance more than Alex.

The duffle slid from her shoulder, landing with a thump on the mud mat. She flattened both palms against the door, and I covered her hands with mine, sliding cool leather over warm skin. I wondered if the gloves worried her, if she sense the danger I posed. I wedged a leg between hers, thigh nudging her ass, and electricity spiked, a current so hot my whole body sizzled. Was she aware of it too? Did she feel my cock prodding her backside?

"You need to leave," she ground out, but even as the words left her mouth, she relaxed in submission. She turned her head and peered at me through lashes slightly lowered, disguising what I might find in her jade depths. "Please, you've gotta go."

I wanted to take her then, fuck her right against the door. "Not a chance. I've waited too long for this." I latched the deadbolt again, satisfied with the decisive click that echoed off the walls, and pulled her further into the house.

"What are you doing?" she cried, tugging against the fingers I'd clamped around her arm.

I stopped once we reached the hall. "Where's the note I left?" I couldn't leave behind any evidence. "Did you show it to Zach?"

She yanked her arm from my grasp. "No, why?"

"Doesn't matter. I want it back."

"It's in my bedroom." She opened the first door on the right. Going by the clothing piled in haphazard fashion on the bed and the floor, she'd packed in a hurry. She crossed to her nightstand and withdrew the note from the drawer.

I snatched it from her fingers, making her flinch, and pocketed the last piece of evidence. "C'mon." I dragged her into the kitchen, my pulse rocketing, and my jeans grew uncomfortably tight as I shoved her into a chair. She gazed up at me, mouth open, messy curls partially obscuring her eyes, and I was so close to bending her over the table.

Patience.

I couldn't rush this, no matter how much I wanted to. "Don't move," I warned, pressing on her shoulders to make my point. I rummaged through the room, found a pen and paper, and slammed them on the table in front of her. "Write down what I say, word for word."

"Why?"

"Quit asking so many fucking questions." I forced the pen into her fingers, and she clutched it tight, hand hovering above the paper. The fury in her eyes wavered, replaced by confusion. She wasn't scared of me yet, and I wasn't sure if that was good or bad.

"Rafe, what are you do—"

"Write 'I need some time. Don't worry or try to find me.'"

Short and to the point. The less written, the less the authorities could dissect. I expected them to look at me as a person of interest in her disappearance, but I was prepared for that inevitability. Besides, they'd need probable cause and a warrant to search the island, and they wouldn't have either.

Lower lip tucked between her teeth, she wrote out the words and paid careful attention to each letter, her hand trembling every so often. Once finished, she set the pen down, angled her head, and met my eyes. She didn't have to voice her alarm. Her expression was unmasked. Naively, she let me see everything.

"What happened to you?" she whispered.

She must have sensed the darkness in me, but what she failed to understand was how it had always lurked, entrapped by a code I no longer lived by. She'd blown the padlock on that cage when she'd uttered three little words that ruined me.

He raped me.

The accusation rang through my mind, as loud as the clank of the prison cell doors when they slammed shut. I grabbed the syringe from my pocket.

"What are you doing?" she cried, wide eyes locking onto the syringe. She jumped into motion and reached the foyer before I caught up to her. I wound an arm around her shoulders and pinned her against me. She bucked, kicked, and clawed, all the while letting loose a scream that made me so fucking hard I almost lost it. I uncapped the needle with my teeth and stabbed it into the side of her neck. An instant later, she went limp in my arms.

3. BREAK ME

ALEX

Consciousness washed over me in dream-like phases, the first a stifling darkness that pressed from every direction. I trembled as an inescapable chill crawled over my skin like icy tendrils, licking with relish. Hard, rough concrete chafed my body. My *naked* body. Acid rose in my throat, and I thought I was about to lose my last meal, but the observation only caused more panic to set in. I couldn't recall what I'd eaten.

For a few horror-stricken moments, I couldn't recall anything at all. Then I remembered.

Rafe's face burned in my head, his older, scruffier face. His unforgiving face. The rest of my memories flooded back, and I jerked to total awareness. He'd jabbed a needle into my neck.

Now, I felt it, his presence casting over me like a shadow waiting to swallow me whole. I tried to throw my hands up, my first instinct one of protection, but something heavy and cold and menacing kept my wrists locked together, stretched behind my head and chained to…something. I whimpered as my brain tried to pound out through my eyeballs.

"Good, you're awake."

His voice shouldn't sound so sexy under the circumstances, but that gravelly timbre, barely above a whisper, registered low in my belly.

"Rafe?" I had to be hallucinating or dead. This couldn't be real.

I sensed movement, a drift of air and swoosh of clothing, and a dim light switched on. Several seconds passed as I blinked my surroundings into focus. I was sprawled on the ground of some sort of cage, my hands secured to the bars. I yanked on my bindings, and the bite of chains to metal made me shudder. My gaze shifted, taking in the space beyond my prison, which was cloaked in shadow, and I thought I spied rows of wine bottles. I returned my attention to him, mouth hanging open as I tried to comprehend that he had me bound and naked.

Rafe stood on the other side and circled the bars with white-knuckled fingers as he glared down at me. "You can try to escape if you want, but I think you're smart enough to know when you're fucked."

On some level, I'd known this day would come. The day I'd have to face him. The day he'd demand an explanation for what I'd done. I'd imagined screaming and yelling on his part. Furious righteousness. Never this. As he withdrew a set of keys and moved to the door of the cage, any hope of forgiveness I'd clung to vanished. I couldn't stop shaking as he stormed inside.

"What do you want from me?" I asked, nervous about the answer, especially when I thought of how my nudity was on display.

"Do you really want to know what I want?" The corner of his mouth turned up in the legendary Rafe Mason smirk I remembered.

"Yes."

He bent and crawled over me, his knees settling at the apex of my thighs, and palmed the concrete on either side of my head. I licked my dry lips, acutely aware of how his clothing tickled my skin. That mere contact, the brush of denim on inner thigh, chased some of the chill away.

"I want to fuck you," he said, and the way those words played off his tongue, with a riff of sinister intent, made my heart jackhammer. His biceps flexed under the strain of supporting his weight, and my attention closed in on the tribal lines streaking out from underneath his sleeves. Breathtaking ink on hard man, winding down strong forearms to the back of his hands. He lowered his face, a tilt to his head, and commanded my gaze. "Is that what you wanted to hear?"

I wasn't sure what I expected him to say or do, and I couldn't begin to measure how angry he was. "I don't know what to say, Rafe."

"You don't have to say anything. I want what's mine, what I served time for."

I gulped. "You didn't have to kidnap me."

"You're right," he said, his lips hovering, almost touching mine. "I didn't have to kidnap you, but I wanted to, and I always get what I want. The last eight fucking years notwithstanding, of course. You made sure of that."

He shifted his weight to the side and brought a key to my wrists. The lock released, and I pulled free of the bars.

"Get up," he said, rising to his feet.

The floor tilted in a dizzying whirl, but once I regained my bearings, I stood before him, face-to-face with the man I'd wronged. He was just as gorgeous as ever, though his green eyes told me things he didn't voice. They hinted at how my actions had ruined a good person, because the one before me was anything but.

My heart ached for the guy I remembered, with his deep laugh and teasing grin. The same mouth that sneered at me now used to curve into the sexiest smile when he caught me staring. I'd fallen hard, enticed by the irresistible contradiction that was Rafe Mason, a guy who displayed a quiet, gentle aura, yet used brute force on his opponents inside the cage. His only crime had been catching the eye of damaged goods.

"Why'd you do it, Alex?" He moved, blocking the opening of the prison and hindering any chance I had to escape.

I wrapped my arms around myself, feeling sick as I recalled the day they arrested him. The media had splashed footage all over the news, and I'd never forget the way his head hung in shame as they hauled him outside my father's gym where he trained, hands cuffed at his back as if he were really guilty. Sometimes, merely being accused of something, even when innocent, could psyche a person into experiencing false guilt. Zach was an expert at that particular mental warfare.

"I asked you a question," he snapped.

The moment had arrived, the one I'd dreaded for years, but my mind drew a blank. What could I tell him? There was no excuse or explanation that would make this right. Even the truth didn't excuse sending an innocent man to prison. "I'm sorry," I said, fighting tears. "You have every right to be angry."

"Are you refusing to give me an explanation? Don't you think I deserve that much?"

I dipped my head, thick hair falling forward and shadowing the shame warming my cheeks. What he deserved was nothing less than the truth, but it caught in my throat, perpetually trapped by my need for him to never find out about Zach and me. "I can't give you one. It won't change anything."

"I see." He came closer, hands bunching at his sides, and ordered me to lower my arms.

I backed up, hating how my body throbbed with indecent anticipation. My eyes burned, but I hadn't cried in a long time, not since my mother died and Rafe had embraced me while I lost it. That seemed like a lifetime ago. I blinked several times, willing the tears to dry up, but the sight of him lowered the gates. Something fundamental in him had changed.

My fault.

My doing.

A tear slipped free. With casual ease, he scooped it up and sucked the moisture off his finger. "Hands at your sides, *now*."

I shook my head, and the gesture probably came off as defiant, but really, I just wanted to crawl into myself and die. The thought of putting my body on display for him sent me into a panic. This body betrayed me, it attracted the wrong attention and glorified in it. All it would take was one touch of his hand for him to realize how I wanted him.

"I-I don't understand."

"What do you not understand, Alex? Sounds pretty clear to me."

"Don't do this," I pleaded, retreating until I bumped into the bars with nowhere to go. I hid myself as much as possible, thighs pressed together and palms covering my breasts.

He unbuckled his belt and pulled it from his jeans.

"Please—" I couldn't breathe, couldn't budge even as adrenaline coursed through me.

"Do as you're told, or I'll make you wish you'd listened the first time."

My arms weren't part of me. Somehow, all on their own, they dropped to my sides like two sticks of deadweight. His eyes traveled over me, starting at my feet and slowly lifting to my belly before roaming higher.

"Look at the set of tits on you."

I stood on a precipice of indecision, and taking the plunge could bring about two different outcomes. Fear, the kind that made your heart beat so fast, your mind tricked you into believing you were seconds from death. Or, I could take a free-fall into insanity. Rafe Mason was, essentially, the love of my life. I could lie to everyone else, but not to myself. Nothing he did would change that.

Even now, as his hand formed an angry fist around that belt, I came alive. Or maybe it was *because* he posed such a threat. God, I was fucked up. I knew what he was capable of. A memory of swollen and bloody flesh sprang to mind, so vividly I could describe it in Technicolor. That last cage fight before they'd arrested him, the one to trump all others, burned in my memory.

His attention lingered on my breasts, and the mere heat of his stare branded me. Here was a man furious, a man few would blame for wanting to do horrible things to the person who'd wrecked his life.

That person was me, and despite the threat in his expression, something about the way he caressed my body with a single glance reduced me to a puddle of need. It pooled between my legs until everything was tight and wet and hot.

With careful patience, he feathered the back of his hand across my nipple, and I felt his touch everywhere, especially between my legs where I ached and burned from the inside out. Until now, I'd never known what it was like to be on the receiving end of Rafe's attention. He was the only guy capable of making me feel this way.

Hot.

Alive.

Needy.

Our gazes entwined, and the feelings spearing through me were too intense to ignore. I'd lost count of the number of fantasies I'd had of this moment when he would touch me. Really touch me. Not as the kid he treated like a sister, not as the bothersome girl who mercilessly drove him to madness, but as a woman.

A woman he wanted.

His hand drifted lower, fingers skimming over

quivering stomach muscles. Breath eluded me. The circumstances mattered no more. Fear evaporated into particles of mist that lingered but weren't powerful enough to douse the feelings I thought I'd buried years ago. All that mattered was his hand, lowering…lowering still. I clenched my thighs to keep from spreading them and braced my back against the bars, hands balled at my sides.

His body pressed into mine, and I closed my eyes, cataloging each sensation from the way his chest flattened my breasts to the heat of his thighs. He lifted my arms above my head and curled my fingers around the bars.

"Don't move," he growled, hands squeezing one last time before falling away. "You are such a fucking tease." His words drifted across my cheek. "I never touched you. No matter how much—" Abruptly, he sprang away as if I'd burned him. "I *never* touched you." He reached for the belt that must have fallen to the concrete. "You destroyed my life," he said, fingers playing with the buckle. "I was *this* close to making it to the UFC, and you snatched it from me." He snapped his fingers. "Just like that, you took my freedom, my reputation. You fucking took everything, Alex. I have to register as a sex offender now? Did you know that?"

"I'm sorr—"

The belt landed across my breasts hard, and I cried out as the breath stole from my lungs. My arms dropped, automatically moving to protect, but he struck again with a powerful crack. I gasped and clung to the bars as my nipples burned.

"Don't you dare tell me you're sorry! You've had eight fucking years to be sorry, but you left me there to rot." The belt slid to his feet, and he kicked my legs apart before shoving a finger inside me.

My eyes grew wide as he probed me, though his jerky thrusts were far from gentle.

"I rotted while you dated that jerk who probably doesn't know the first thing about setting you off." He added three more fingers, wrecking my concentration, his touch stretching and reaching higher. "Did he make you feel this good?"

I squeezed my eyes shut and began counting. Five in, hold, five out. Repeat.

"Answer me!"

"He didn't." Lucas' kisses and wandering hands had made me feel nothing, but Rafe…he made me feel everything. I swallowed past the self-loathing constricting my throat, tried to ignore the slippery plunder of his fingers, but a strangled moan escaped anyway.

"Do you want me to stop?"

Yes.

"No." I extended to my toes, fingers gripping the bars for support, and barely breathed as his thumb rubbed circles on my clit. "Rafe!" I pushed my pelvis against his hand even as tears leaked down my face. His mouth opened over my throat, and I inhaled sharply, my pulse throbbing an erratic beat underneath his tongue.

This wasn't happening. My body wasn't betraying me again. No, no, no, no…

"I still remember how to touch a woman," he said. "I bet my fingers are the best fuck you've had. Can you imagine my tongue on your pussy?" He licked up my throat, and I whimpered, imagining it all too well. I saw myself on my back, legs spread wide and his dark head disappearing between quaking thighs. The visual was too much, and I hurtled into deep space. I saw the celestial heavens.

"I'm coming," I sobbed.

"Yes, you are, sweetheart. Enjoy it because it won't happen again."

I clawed at his dark T-shirt, my spine bowing and knees threatening to give. The orgasm came in waves around his fingers, each one more intense than the last, and each one filled my heart with so much shame my chest was heavy with it. Riding the waves, I howled his name, my cries resembling a cat in the throes. Afterward, as my heartbeat slowed, I collapsed to the floor.

"You're at my mercy," he said, crouching to eye level. "You don't eat unless I allow it, you don't drink. You don't get clothes or a shower or even a bed to sleep in unless I say so. I control every piece of you, including your fucking pussy." I wrenched my head to the side, pained by the hardened features of his beautiful face, but he pressed his fingers into my jaw and forced me to meet his gaze. "You're going to earn every damn privilege known to man. Do you understand me?"

"Yes." The force of his fury penetrated deep, and I would have agreed to anything in that moment.

"You are nothing to me, Alex. You will never be more than a piece of ass." My heart cracked as he let go, forming a jagged chasm I feared would forever remain. I watched him walk away, tears sliding down my cheeks, one after the other in an endless stream of regret. He exited the prison without looking back and the lock clicked into place with an unsettling echo. He bent to retrieve a pile of neatly folded clothing—my clothing, by the looks of it—and then climbed a staircase. An instant later, the light shut off.

Total blackness.

I couldn't stop crying. Not because I was scared. Not because he'd just humiliated me. I muffled heaving sobs into my palms because his utter contempt sliced to my soul. And now I knew.

He was going to break me.

4. THE CODE

RAFE

I'd just lied through my fucking teeth. She did mean something, which was why she was down in that prison. If she meant nothing, I wouldn't have wanted her in the first place. The musky scent of her sex lingered on my skin, and I sucked a finger into my mouth, unable to resist tasting her. I couldn't wait to spread those thighs, thumbs biting into soft skin, and bury my tongue in her heat.

Before she sent me away, I'd done my damnedest to do the honorable thing by keeping my distance, though there'd been times I'd slipped up. Like the time she baited me into a game of pool by implying she was unbeatable. We'd played a fiercely competitive game, all the while bantering about horror movies and alternative rock music.

She loved the horror and loathed the rock. Not surprising, since she adored the piano.

I'd smoked her the first game. During the second, she conceded and asked for my help in positioning her for the end shot. That was the first time I acknowledged the familiar tingle rushing through me as I bent over her, my hand sliding along hers and guiding her to set up the shot that would win her the game.

I'd also realized, too late, how she'd used the game as a ploy to get close to me. We'd both jumped a foot apart when Zach's boots thumped down the stairs, and our faces must have given us away because he was furious. The protective thumb he held over her wasn't new. Guys couldn't go near her without him losing it, but he should have known better when it came to me. Beyond helping her with a game of pool, I would have never crossed that line. Twenty-one and fifteen didn't mix.

I didn't touch her again, until the day, a few weeks later, when she had a total meltdown after her mom's funeral. I'd needed her in my arms, needed to absorb some of her pain.

Leaning my head against the cellar door, I let my breath even out as a tremor seized my body, and the memory of our history together vanished. I fought the urge to go back down there and finish what I'd started. My dick throbbed with the need, though I held back. I was still too fucking raw, and I didn't want to make the kind of mistake that proved fatal. With the visual I had going through my mind—hands wrapped around her delicate throat as I emptied eight years of pent-up rage and desire into her—I knew I couldn't rush this. Control was imperative.

But shit, I wanted to fuck her.

I waited, listening for a while, but she didn't make a sound, and I had to give her credit. I'd left her in total darkness, naked, and no doubt, freezing. These next few days were going to be hell compared to her pampered princess life.

I'd scared the utter crap out of her, and some sick part of me rejoiced in reducing her to nothing. She didn't even have a bucket to piss in. Watching her cower had been the biggest rush of my life, and that was saying a lot, considering I used to live for pummeling bodies inside the cage.

Maybe it was because I'd fixated on her in prison. At first, nothing but hatred consumed me, but then as my incarceration started playing with my mind, I'd let my imagination run wild. I'd fucked her every way possible, and in each scenario, she'd sobbed and pleaded for me to stop. I'd envisioned sexually torturing her in ways no sane, normal man should be able put into words.

Those fantasies kept me on the brink of sanity, especially during the endless weeks I'd spent in the hole, bereft of interaction with humans and confined to a dark cell smaller than most bathrooms for twenty-three hours a day.

When I looked in the mirror these days, I didn't recognize the man staring back. The guy who'd wiped the sorrow from her face the day she buried her mother, absorbing liquid grief that dripped from her eyes in torrents of despair, was gone, replaced by a man who thrilled in eliciting her tears. Darkness turned at the core of my being, a turbulent need that had simmered for years.

No one knew of my fucked up nature better than my old cellmate Jax. As I entered the kitchen, her clothes weighing heavily in my hands, he watched me carefully from the kitchen table as I disposed of them.

"Did you fuck her yet?" That was the thing I liked most about him—he didn't beat around the bush. He put everything out there without reservation.

As I prepared dinner, I didn't answer, and he didn't speak at first. His silence wasn't uncomfortable. We'd spent hours upon hours in the same cell with nothing but silence and each other.

We'd forged an alliance after I'd beaten the shit out of his would-be killer in prison. He owed me, or so he insisted, and when they paroled him two years ago, he'd set out to repay the debt by keeping tabs on Alex. He'd also taken care of the island since the deed transferred to my name. In exchange, I gave him a place to live.

After last night, I considered the debt more than paid. He'd helped drag Alex's limp body from her car to mine, then we'd shared a minute of silence as we watched her Volvo sink into the river.

"Well, did ya?" he pressed, breaking into my recollection of how satisfying it'd been to follow through with my plan.

I gave him a single glance, and he laughed.

"Man, you're whipped. I can't believe you didn't fuck her yet."

"I didn't say a word, so how do you know if I fucked her or not?"

"I know you," he said, pushing his dark blond hair back from his forehead. "You go all quiet and shit when you don't wanna talk. Alex De Luca has been our topic of choice for years. What the fuck is the holdup, man?"

"I don't know. I can't go there yet." I dropped my head with a sigh. Going where I wanted to go would probably turn what was left of me to stone.

"'Cause you're not a rapist. I told you so. No way can you do that to her. Not after what you've been through."

"No, believe me—I *want* to go there." I returned my attention to the oven and slid the chicken onto the rack. "She wanted it too much."

"You want her to put up a fight?"

Blood rushed to my cock, confirming his theory. "I'm fucking whacked."

"No, you just want payback. Ain't nothing wrong with that."

Thanks to Alex, I knew firsthand what it was like to be helpless, though I hadn't made a single sound of defeat once in the last eight years. Not when they closed the bars on me for something I didn't do, not when other inmates jumped me, held me down, and took turns ramming into my ass. Not even when my father died and I'd been denied the chance to go to his funeral.

I hated to consider what he'd think of me now, how much shame calling me his son would bring him. I'd taken the island he'd willed to me, the one place I equated with happy summertime memories during my childhood, and had turned it into my own personal Alcatraz.

No amount of guilt or shame would change what I wanted most—to unleash the same torment I'd experienced on my single prisoner. The way she looked at me though, the way she responded, really pissed me off. I wanted a fight. I wanted her fingernails digging into me. I wanted her kicking and screaming and begging for mercy. I wanted her tears *and* her fucking pain. "Payback is one thing, but the things I want to do to her…"

Jax settled his chin in his hand, and a wide grin split his face. "Have you forgotten we used to jack off in the same cell? You also talk in your sleep. I know what you want to do to that girl. I just never thought you'd have the balls to go through with it."

"Trust me, my balls aren't the problem. And she's not a girl anymore."

"All the better. What are you waiting for? Go fuck her rough-like. Find the right buttons and push the fuck outta them. Hell, if you don't want her, I'll take her."

He only said it to goad me, and it worked. "Stay away from her," I said with a growl.

Jax held up his hands. "'Nough said. I'm a firm believer in the code."

"What code?"

"The leave-my-woman-the-fuck-alone code. You want her? She's all yours." He pushed up from the table. "I've gotta be back in town." He paused with a wicked grin. "Got plans tonight."

"Seriously?" I arched a brow, surprised because Jax had issues when it came to women. Being with a woman usually involved physical contact, and he couldn't stand to be touched.

"Plans as in a date?"

"Uh-huh."

"With a woman?"

He leveled me with a stare. "Yes, with a *woman*."

"Hey, I'm just surprised, is all. Whatever gets you out there, man."

"Goes both ways. You need to get down there and fuck her senseless. Eight years is a long time to wait."

Shit. He was good at turning a conversation on its

head.

He lifted his jacket off the back of the chair. "Gotta work tomorrow, so I won't be too late."

My brother Adam had given Jax a job when no one else in the area would touch a felon. I also put in hours at Mason Vineyards, but it was mostly to uphold the illusion I was a positive contributing citizen. I didn't need to work, thanks to my inheritance. However, idleness drove me nuts, made me want to rip into something, and Alex had ruined my career as a fighter, so working off steam the way I used to wasn't an option. A punching bag didn't deliver the same gratifying release as pounding flesh. Since I'd taken her though, my presence at the winery was about to become nonexistent, at least for a while.

"Seriously, Rafe. Fuck the shit outta her."

"Is that an order?"

"Damn right. You've earned a piece of that."

I was one sick SOB because I felt he was right.

5. DISORDERLY

ALEX

The first time I saw Rafe Mason, he was beating the crap out of my brother. Okay, that was an exaggeration, but watching through the inexperienced eyes of a 13-year-old, even I'd realized Zach didn't stand a chance.

Rafe was all rippling muscle, sweat dripping down his biceps as he tightened his choke hold. Let me back up here. They hadn't *really* been fighting. They'd been in the middle of an intense sparring match at one of the gyms our father owned. Fuck if I'd cared though. I couldn't take my eyes off Rafe. His dark and wild hair, plastered to his forehead from sweat, had curled slightly above squinted green eyes. I remembered Mom's stiff posture and the rigid set of her back as we stood watching. Her mouth had fallen open, as if she were *this* close to shouting "let him go!" We'd come in on the tail end of the session, and Mom should have known better. She never could stomach watching Zach get his balls handed to him.

Rafe hadn't just handed them over—he'd shoved them down his throat. That was the day he and Zach became best friends. Predictably so, that was also the day I developed the biggest crush on Rafe.

By the time I entered my freshman year of high school, I became Miss Popularity because of two reasons: one, I was a De Luca—the adopted daughter of Abbot De Luca, famous for his impressive record in the UFC; and two, I was sister to rising star Zachariah De Luca. Having a connection to Rafe Mason, who had surpassed my brother in skill, tenacity, and ruthlessness in the business sealed my fate. I became an "it" girl.

I hated "it" girls, but they didn't seem fazed by my blatant indifference, as not one of them passed up an opportunity to hang out at my house. They were in it for the testosterone, and I didn't really care, so long as they kept their hands off Rafe. He might have been six years my senior, but in my head, he was mine, though someone forgot to tell him.

However, Zach noticed me noticing his best friend, and that's when the jealousy began, the dangerous possessiveness. Their friendship had shifted to more of a competitive nature.

Ever since our parents married, Zach and I had been tight, probably closer than most blood related siblings. We often slept in the same bed, huddled under the covers when Dad's drinking got out of hand, or when my mom had another episodic break that necessitated a trip to the mental ward. Their marriage had crumbled under screams that pierced ears too young to understand the words being launched through the air like weapons of mass destruction.

Having Zach at my side calmed me, but as I grew older, I realized how off our relationship was, especially once Rafe's presence got under Zach's skin, and my brother had morphed into a stranger before my eyes.

The police arrested the wrong guy, and I let them.

In hindsight, I had no one to blame but myself for my current predicament—naked and freezing, ass chafed from the concrete, utterly humiliated. I almost pissed myself every time something scampered in the darkness. How silly to be scared of rodents when a man I once knew so well held me prisoner.

A door opened unexpectedly, and the overhead light came on. I squinted, the dim bulb too bright on eyes accustomed to nothing but suppressing blackness. Rafe stomped down the stairs and halted outside the cage.

I couldn't say how much time had passed since I'd awakened in this hellhole, but if I had to guess by the coarse hair on my legs, the smell of unbathed skin, and the tangled, greasy mess on my head, I'd say about three days. I'd lost count of his visits. The first was the most notable, as he'd tossed a bucket to the ground for me to do my business in, left a tray of food and a bottle of water next to it, and exited without a single response to my pleas. The visits that followed wielded the same results, and I stopped begging, accepting I might be down here for a while.

Crouched in the corner, I draped my arms around shaking legs. "I-I'm cold," I said through chattering teeth. "Can I have a blanket? Please?"

He unlocked the door and sauntered inside. "I spent weeks in the hole, naked just like you. Do you think I got a blanket?" He knelt and lifted my chin. "I usually got a beat down before they threw me in, and some days, they didn't even feed me." His mouth flattened into a grim line. "Lucky for you, I'm not as nasty as the guards who had it out for me."

I stared, overcome by the guilt that chiseled off another piece of my heart. I wished I could comfort him, erase the last eight years. What an impossible idea.

"What do you want with me?" I asked. "Do you want to hurt me? Fuck me?" Whatever he was going to do, I hoped he'd just do it. The waiting made me a nervous wreck.

"You took eight years of my life. I think it's only fair I

take eight of yours."

I couldn't believe what I was hearing. His words turned in the pit of my stomach like acid. "You're going to keep me here for eight years?"

He tightened his hold on my chin. "Are you hungry?"

His refusal to answer didn't escape me. Something felt different about this visit. He was deviating from his routine, and I wasn't sure what it meant. The thought of eating made me nauseous, but I wasn't about to argue with him. Maybe he'd finally let me out.

"Yes. I need to use the restroom too." I prayed he wouldn't make me use the disgusting bucket again. Even from the other side of the cell, the stench of port-a-potty contaminated the air.

He stepped back and gestured toward that awful thing. "Better go then."

I climbed to my feet and stretched the deep ache from my body, then I suffered the indignity of squatting over the bucket while he watched, inked arms crossed as a corner of his mouth turned up. Once I'd relieved my bladder, I stood, unsure of where to put my hands. If I folded them over my chest, I might anger him, so I let them dangle at my sides.

"Follow me," he said, "and don't do anything stupid unless you want to end up back down here."

I scurried up the stairs after him, each step landing with uncertainty. We entered a large kitchen where a burst of sunshine streamed through the skylight. Dark clouds roiled, a sign another storm threatened on the horizon and the rays were only a temporary reprieve. I searched the area beyond the windows and found thick and sodden greenery outside. A door off the kitchen drew my attention, and I wondered what my odds were of making it outside before he grabbed me.

I was peeking into the adjacent living room, as the cabin took advantage of an open floor plan, when he said, "You reek. Shower's that way." He indicated a bathroom straight ahead and to the left of the dining table. "Towel's on the rack. You've got five minutes before I come in after you."

I hurried inside and plopped down on the toilet, shaking too much to do anything else. I lowered my head between my knees and breathed deep. Five in, hold, five out. Repeat. By the time I stood on jittery legs, I'd lost at least two of my five minutes. Another thirty seconds passed as I puzzled over how to escape, but the bathroom was a windowless cubicle with no way out. As I switched on the shower and stepped inside the stall, I wondered where I'd go if I did manage to break free. I'd been an instant away from leaving my house, duffle packed, when he'd shown up. How stupid, considering I hadn't put together even the flimsiest of plans, and if Zach ever tracked me down…I didn't want to think of how he'd punish me for running.

A shiver went through me, and I quickly washed up before drying off with a towel. Despite spending the last few days in the nude, exiting the bathroom sans-clothing felt exceptionally violating. I finger-combed some of the tangles from my dark locks and returned to the dining area.

Rafe had his back to me, bent over with his head in the refrigerator, and I almost ran for it, except fear of what he'd do if I failed paralyzed me. But the real reason I didn't run was harder to stomach. I wasn't ready to leave. Some masochistic shred of my being didn't want to walk away from him yet, even though staying defied logic and common sense.

Reality check, Alex. He's kidnapped you, drugged you, and he's obviously not right in the head. Run for it, stupid!

But running for it meant arriving back at square one. Still, my pride wouldn't let me lay down without a fight. "My father will find me."

He pulled out a carton of orange juice and turned around. "No one's looking for you, so you might as well take a seat and get comfortable."

I folded my arms. "You should know better. You spent enough time with my dad. You know how dogged he can be." Especially when it came to his kids, Zach in particular.

Setting the juice down, he picked up a paper and shoved it across the table. Slowly, and with worsening dread gnawing my gut, I picked it up and read the headline:

Portland woman declared dead after car is found in the Columbia River.

I collapsed into a chair, thoughts buzzing in dizzying speed, and the paper fluttered to the table. Dad and I often navigated a rocky relationship, but even so, the news would devastate him, and Zach would go insane knowing I was gone.

Wait…he thought I was dead.

Seconds slipped by as the ramifications sank in, and I worked it from every angle. If he believed I'd been killed, then he'd have no reason to come after me, and no reason to go after Rafe.

But that still didn't give Rafe the right to keep me here and torture me. "You have to let me go." Surely, he didn't intend to keep me locked in this cabin, or God forbid, the horrible cellar, for eight years.

"You're not going anywhere," he said through clenched teeth, "so get that through your head."

"The guy I remember would never do this."

"The guy you remember is as gone as you are to the world." He yanked me up by my wet hair. "You can either learn that the easy way or the hard way."

"And this is the hard way?" I asked, flinching as his

fingers tightened. "Kidnapping me? Stripping me? Locking me up?"

"You sent me to hell, Alex. I'm just returning the favor."

He let go, and I sank into my seat again as his words echoed through my heart. "Will you at least give my clothes back? *Please*," I begged, sliding my hands under my thighs, as the urge to cover myself nearly overpowered me.

His gaze settled on my breasts, and I felt my nipples harden. "I like the view. Eight years is a long time to go without seeing a pair of tits. You'll get clothes when I'm good and ready." He set a plate of food in front of me, and the smell of scrambled eggs, something that had always reminded me of wet dog when I cooked them, turned my stomach.

"I'm not hungry."

He sat across from me, his own plate in front of him. "It's not optional. Eat your damn food."

Rage erupted from me, refusing to be contained, and I had to act, had to do something, if only to alleviate the madness festering inside me. I knocked the plate off the table, and though I was disappointed it failed to shatter, the way the food spattered the floor gave some satisfaction.

He rubbed the stubble that shadowed his jaw, as if contemplating, and rose from his chair. He rounded the table, furious green eyes narrowed, and I grabbed my seat to keep from bolting. Oh God. I'd never been more sorry about losing my temper. He settled next to me, and I couldn't comprehend what happened next. One second I was sitting upright, and the next he'd pulled me over his lap.

His palm came down fast and hard, but I didn't make a sound, didn't even fight him. I was too shocked, too aware of him underneath me as his thighs burned into my abdomen. His hand stalled on my ass, lightly massaging, then he continued spanking me, each smack landing with more intensity than the last. He set me upright again, and only then did I register the deep sting in my bottom. He reclaimed the seat across from me, and I opened my mouth but nothing came out.

All I could do was stare. There were no words, no fits or hysterics, just pure stunned silence on my part.

"If you think a tantrum will get you out of eating, you're sorely mistaken." He pointed at my breakfast on the floor. "Get down there and eat it."

"I'm not a fucking dog."

He jumped from his chair so fast, I didn't have a chance to bolt. His fingers pressed into my jaw. "Last chance before I use *that* on you." He forced my gaze to the thick paddle hanging on the wall by the door. "And trust me, that sucker is unbearable, so unless you want to experience it firsthand, get your ass on the floor and eat your breakfast. I won't tolerate you starving yourself. Not under my roof."

Warmth flooded my face as I slid from the chair to my knees, and as I used my hands to shovel in mouthfuls of eggs, the same old shame surfaced. It was never far, always hidden beneath layers of forged normalcy. "I haven't had a problem with that in six months," I said, despising the weak quality of my voice. The eggs didn't want to go down, and I almost gagged. The potatoes weren't much better.

"Good, and we're going to keep it that way."

"How did you know?" I asked. He'd just been released from prison, so how had he found out about my problem with anorexia?

"I know everything about you."

Our eyes connected and held, and I searched for the truth, because surely he didn't mean *everything.* Seconds ticked past, each one whittling away my thin grasp on sanity. I held my breath, horrified by the possibility that he *knew.*

He broke our stare, his expression unchanged, and I exhaled in relief. Silence ensued, interrupted by the scrape of his fork against china, but it wasn't the uncomfortable kind of disquiet that made every second feel like an eternity. My mind was numb. I hadn't processed, and I wasn't ready to do so.

"Why did you starve yourself?" he asked, jerking me

to awareness.

I had no idea how to explain. I couldn't explain, not without going into things I didn't want to reveal, like how after the first inpatient treatment, I'd relapsed on purpose because being locked inside that facility had been the most peaceful three months I'd experienced in a long time. My treatment had kept Zach away. "I don't know."

"Bullshit."

I scooped up a handful of potatoes. "It started after…" I began, raising my eyes to his, "after you went away."

"Your eating disorder is my fault then?"

"No, that's not what I meant. I was dealing with a lot of stuff and—"

"Save it, Alex. I'm sure you were really struggling in your daddy's mansion, going out on the weekends with boyfriends and friends, loading up your closets with expensive clothes. Spare me the sob story, 'cause I'm not buying."

"Why'd you ask then?" With a tilt of my head, I raised my brows.

"Don't get smart with me. I thought you might actually tell the truth for once in your life." He pushed back from the table. "Clear the table and load the dishwasher." He swept a hand toward the messy floor. "And clean up this mess."

Indignation rose, but I kept my mouth shut. Rising to

my feet, I grabbed my plate from the floor and his from the table before making my way to the sink. I took my time scrubbing the few dishes from breakfast, and after I'd loaded them into the dishwasher, I slammed the door, turned around, and found him watching me. He was leaning against the counter, arms crossed and biceps bulging.

"I need a broom."

He fetched one from a closet near the door leading to God knew where. Where the hell had he taken me? I saw nothing but trees, though the distinct hum of a highway gave me hope that help existed beyond all the thick foliage.

He shoved the broom into my hands, and our fingers brushed together—the kind of touch that lingered enough to make me shiver. I swallowed hard and swept up the mess, sensing him behind me the whole time. His warm palms settled on my hips, fingers curling around to my front. I swayed into his body.

"Can…can I ask you something, Rafe?"

"You can ask."

"Have you…" My voice faltered, and I had to swallow hard in order to force the question out. "Have you had sex since getting out?"

He trembled. "No," he groaned as he dipped a finger inside me, and I quaked at the thought that he hadn't been with anyone in such a long time.

"Now it's my turn to ask you something," he said. "Just how badly do you want me to fuck you?"

A whimper escaped. It was no secret my body wanted him, had always wanted him. But me, the woman he'd kidnapped, she *didn't* want him. That's what I told myself, anyway.

"You wanted it back then too." With a growl, he pushed me away. "I don't want you like this."

"What's that supposed to mean?" I turned to face him, the broom handle keeping me upright.

"It means I don't want you willing." He knocked the broom to the floor and gripped my wrists. In the rays of the sun peeking through the skylight, my scars stood out as lines of abstract art on my forearms, sketched in blood by my inability to cope with stress. He pulled out my arms and put the marred skin on display.

"What the hell happened to you?"

"Nothing," I said, trying to pull away, but he wouldn't let me.

"Who did this?"

"No one."

He jerked me close, and his immovable hands framed my cheeks. "Who. Did. This?"

"I did."

For the first time since he'd re-entered my life, he appeared speechless. His gaze scoured my face, as if looking for answers.

"Why?"

I shook my head, unable to speak, scared he'd see too much. But I couldn't look away. I didn't want to look away. I wanted to bathe in the gentleness breaking through in that instant when I glimpsed the old Rafe.

He blinked and the moment shattered, his emotions going into lockdown. Without another word, he dragged me toward the cellar.

"Don't put me back down there," I pleaded.

He flung open the door and herded me down the stairs. I was shaking too much to fight. Back in the cage, he fastened shackles around my wrists and jerked my arms high, attaching the chain to a hook in the ceiling. "This should keep you out of trouble for a while." He held my chin, fingers bruising my jaw. "Every time you rebel, this is where you'll end up. Learn to obey me, and we'll get along fine."

And that's how he left me. Alone, cold, and in the dark, with my arms suspended above my head.

6. SPAWN

RAFE

Dante's Pass, population 893, and half of them thought I was guilty as fuck. The place still felt like home, in spite of the busybodies who wanted to see me rot in jail until I was nothing but bones for what I'd done to that "poor girl." They were the ones who sneered at my reputation as Rafe "The Choker" Mason from my fighting days. They were the ones who sensed something was off about me.

But others, mostly people who'd had connections to my family for decades, or people who'd known me in high school, they believed I was innocent. Unlike the crowd that condemned me, they saw past Alex's lie. They *knew* me, or so they believed.

Either way, it was too much drama, so I avoided town

as much as possible, save for the weekly trip to the post office and my work at the vineyard. Despite the town gossip, people mostly left me alone. I imagined it was difficult to harass a guy on an island.

As I sorted through a stack of mail, mostly bills and advertisements, someone uttered my name. Locking the P.O. Box, I swiveled my head in time to see a blonde whirl around and push the door open. She grabbed the hand of the kid at her side and ushered him outdoors, as if the place were about to burn to the ground.

I folded my mail inside an advertisement for local businesses and glanced through the front window, catching the woman's profile as she walked away. My heart almost stopped. I'd recognize that stubborn jaw anywhere. I rushed after her, the door closing with a thud upon my exit, and spotted her a few feet down the sidewalk. She opened the back door of a white BMW, and in hushed tones, hurried the kid to get inside and buckle up.

"Nikki!"

She lurched upright, and her deep, brown eyes met mine. Yeah, I remembered those eyes, especially how they bored into mine during sex. Nikki had never been the shy closed-eyes-during-sex kind of girl, and that had been the biggest turn-on.

She slammed the door and rounded the hood to the driver's side. "I heard you were back," she said. "Seeing you caught me off guard. I shouldn't have said your name."

I stuffed the mail into my back pocket and sauntered to her side. "Why the hell not?"

With a sigh, she paused, one hand on the door handle. "C'mon, things didn't end well. You made it clear you never wanted to see me again."

"Nik," I said, voice suddenly wobbly as I slid a hand onto her shoulder. I had to touch her. After eight damn years, I needed to. "I didn't want you waiting around for me."

She opened the door and wedged it between us. "Well, I didn't wait around, so you have nothing to worry about." She held out her left hand, and my eyes widened at the huge rock on her finger. "I'm getting married in a few weeks."

It was disconcerting to see how much things had changed while I was away. While time had all but stopped inside that prison, the world kept turning without me. "So I see," I said, giving in to a weak instance of self-pity. I moved around the door and put one hand on the window and the other on the roof of the car. Her body stilled, but she had nowhere to go, and shit, just being this close to her brought everything back, all the summer nights we'd spent twisted in sheets, fan blowing hot air on bodies slick with sweat.

"I didn't realize you were back in town," I said.

"Figured you worked in some swanky office in downtown Portland by now. When did you come back?"

"Last year, when Lyle asked me to marry him."

I quirked a brow. "Wait, you're not talking about Lyle Lewis."

She nodded.

I tried not to grit my teeth but failed. How the fuck had that asswipe gotten tangled with my ex? He'd followed her around like a horn dog all through high school, and that was only half of it. The guy had been the cruelest bully in town, and he'd hated me down to my toes for looking out for a few of the kids he'd abused on a daily basis. He'd also despised me because of my friendship with Nikki.

"You know he's the sheriff now, right?" she asked.

Wonderful. She was marrying a fucking bully-turned-sheriff. If I didn't get Alex under control soon, he might be slapping cuffs on me in the future, and I could only imagine the thrill he'd get at arresting me.

"I guess congratulations are in order." I tilted my head, one brow raised.

"I guess so," she said, her gaze veering to the backseat of the car. "I've really gotta go. It was good to see you again, Rafe." Her voice softened, the same breathless quality I recalled from years ago. She slid into the driver's seat, and that was when the kid in the back called her "Mom" and asked what they were having for dinner.

I froze as it dawned on me. I'd been so focused on Nikki, part of me still thinking of her as the twenty-year-old girl I'd known, that I'd unconsciously written the kid off as a nephew, or perhaps a child of a friend.

But he was *hers*.

As she moved to pull the door shut, I shot out a hand and blocked her. Peeking into the backseat, I laid eyes on the kid for the first time. Really looked at him. Fuck. He was a spitting image of my childhood photos.

"How old is he, Nikki?"

Her body slumped, and with a loud sigh, she said, "Seven, and I know what you're thinking. I was going to tell you. Swear to God I was, but now is not the time." Her eyes pleaded with me. "Can we meet for dinner? In about an hour?"

I couldn't speak at first. I could have said so many things, but the truth hit me like a sledgehammer. Unless I was reading her wrong, or misunderstanding, she was telling me I had a son.

"Rafe?"

"An hour?" I asked, giving myself a mental shake.

"Yeah, I'll meet you at Doc's Grill. You remember where that is, right?"

"I remember."

She pulled the door shut, and this time I let her. I stood frozen in that spot long after she pulled away from the curb, the kid's green eyes burning a hole in my mind.

His curious eyes that reminded me so much of my own. Had he seen it too, or was he too young to pick up on the resemblance?

Someone jostled me to awareness, and from the pinch of disproval on the woman's face, she must have been in the "he should rot in prison" camp.

"Sorry," I mumbled, then shook my head because I'd just apologized to a judgmental broad for simply standing in public. Fuck these people. I wandered down the main drag of the town until I reached the highway and stepped onto the shoulder. Checking my watch, I began walking to kill time before I met up with Nikki. The idea of that meeting sent my pulse racing. I wondered what he was like. Had he asked about me?

Hell, I didn't even know his name.

Behind me, the sun dipped toward the horizon, and the shadow of the island emerged in the river up ahead. The private piece of land, situated on the Oregon side of the Columbia River, had been in my family for generations. My mother split when I was young, and my anger over her absence had slowly burned until it flared during my teens. Dad tried to stem my violent tendencies by enrolling me into martial arts classes. He'd thought if I learned to fight with respect and a code of ethics, it would curb my thirst to pound on people. It wasn't like I'd gone around beating on everyone, just the idiots who deserved it, but he'd had the right idea. Those lessons had probably saved my ass.

I wondered if my son—even thinking of him as mine set my head spinning—was angry over the gaping hole I should have filled all these years. Cars whizzed past, and for some strange reason, the hum of traffic settled my nerves. The island grew larger as the distance narrowed. I put the issue of fatherhood on the back burner and wondered how Alex was handling being locked up in the dark, her naked body shivering. I imagined her legs shaking, thought of how out-of-control she must feel, strung up on her toes and knowing she was at my mercy. My jeans grew unbearably tight.

Such helplessness shouldn't turn me on so fucking much, but it did. Always had. My dad's efforts to teach me right from wrong hadn't touched on sexual deviance.

The mountains had turned to dusky blue against an orange backdrop by the time I turned around and retraced my steps back to town. Doc's Grill, known for their unique dishes and secret sauces that couldn't be duplicated anywhere else, was boisterous with activity. The restaurant had never suffered for business. That hadn't changed in my absence, though so much about the town had, like the remodeled school, or how the post office no longer shared space with Cathy's Quik-N-Go.

I entered, nodded at the waitress, and told her I was there to meet someone. I found Nikki sitting by herself at a corner table, nursing a beer. Candles lit the wooden tables, giving an intimate feel to the place, though the peanut shells covering the floor spoke of the casual setting.

I slid into the chair across from her. "Sorry I'm late." I'd lost track of time, plus, I'd needed several minutes to convince my dick to settle down. No way was I walking in to meet Nikki with a raging hard-on.

"No problem. I was enjoying the quiet. William can be a handful, and I don't get much 'me' time."

"William?"

She dipped her head, and a curtain of blond hair obscured the left side of her face. "I named him after you."

William, my middle name. How was it possible I'd had a son all this time, one who shared my name even, yet I'd known nothing about him? Seven years of missed birthdays, milestones, laughter and tears.

Thankfully, the waitress arrived to take our orders, and as Nikki asked about the daily specials, I took a few seconds to collect myself. I was a father. A dad. I had a kid. If I told myself that enough times, maybe it would sink in.

The waitress, a young brunette on the short side, turned to me and did a double take. "I thought you looked familiar. You're Rafe Mason. My boyfriend is a huge fan. He never believed you raped that girl." She winked at me. "A lot of people around here don't."

Unfortunately, a lot of people still did.

I autographed a napkin for her and gave her my order. Once she left, thick silence fell over us.

Time to rip off the Band-Aid. "You should've told me, Nik."

"What good would it have done?" She leaned back and crossed her arms. "You were locked up, and you weren't getting out anytime soon. Besides, let's not delude ourselves. We were never serious. Getting pregnant…it just happened. I can't say it was a mistake because I wouldn't have William, but we never meant for it to happen."

I picked up a spoon and swirled the ice chips in my water glass. "I actually thought I'd marry you someday."

She laughed. "C'mon, Rafe. We were kids back then."

And now we had a kid together. Neither of us spoke the words, though they hung in the air, as potent as the spices from the restaurant's kitchen.

"We both know someday wouldn't have come," she continued. "You had your whole career in front of you before…" She lowered her head, and I despised how she didn't say the words.

"Do you think I did it?"

"I told you a long time ago I knew you wouldn't do something like that." The corner of her mouth curled. "You never needed to force yourself on anyone. You had women begging at your feet."

I tried not to squirm in my seat. Ironically, I had a naked woman, bound and locked up at that precise moment, just waiting for me to hold her down and fuck her hard. Nikki had no idea who I was. Who I'd become. She should have, though. She'd been the only woman who'd ever allowed me to get rough with her. I'd explored some of my baser urges with her, and she'd let me. She'd gotten off on it as much as I had. That's why we'd worked. Our deep friendship had kept the drama to a minimum. We truly had been friends with benefits. Until I was arrested.

And now, to find out my relationship with her had resulted in a kid…

"What did you tell him about me?"

"The truth. I've always wanted you to be part of his life. Eight years seemed like forever to you, but I knew you'd get out eventually." She brushed her bangs from her eyes—eyes suddenly bright. "I didn't want to make things worse for you in there, so I kept quiet about the pregnancy."

Ah, shit. I hated when chicks cried. Except for Alex. Her tears affected me differently. I craved them. "It's water under the bridge. I'm here now, so let's deal with this. You told him his dad went to prison?"

She shook her head. "I told him you had to go away for a few years, but you'd come back when you could. He's at that age now where vague answers aren't cutting it anymore. He wants to meet his father, Rafe."

This was unbelievable, and bad fucking timing. I'd just committed a felony—for real this time—and I was about to compound felony upon felony. I couldn't stop what I'd started, especially now. If I let Alex go, she'd run straight to the cops.

What a fucking mess. I pushed back from the table and resisted the urge to grab at my collar. "I need some time."

"I understand."

"No, I don't think you do. Nik…I've done things. Things I can't undo. I'm not the same guy I was eight years ago."

"I realize that."

"No, you don't." Sighing, I ran a hand through my hair and pulled at the strands until my scalp burned. "You should've told me. You should've fucking told me."

I tossed a few bills onto the table to cover the dinner I wouldn't eat, and then I rushed from the restaurant like the coward I was. But the question remained; if she *had* told me, would it have changed my mind about taking Alex?

7. FIRST TIME

ALEX

I wanted to die.

I didn't know how long he'd left me suspended, but it was messing with my head. I'd lost all sense of time and direction. My body was numb, almost weightless, except for the burn that circled my wrists. That pain didn't go away, no matter how much I tried to block it out. At some point, I started counting...at some point I'd also given up. By the time 7,200 seconds passed, I was about to go out of my mind. The time after that was endless. My voice had gone hoarse long ago from screaming his name.

He never came, and I began to panic. Maybe the past eight years had made him snap and tormenting me this way was his only source of relief. Images popped into my mind, scenarios of him beaten in prison, or worse. The helplessness he must have experienced, just as I was now. I tried to wrap my mind around eight years, but I could hardly wrap my mind around the few hours since he'd slammed the door shut, once again leaving me in darkness. A sick feeling formed in my gut.

God, he must really hate me. My actions, born of cowardice and shame, had labeled him a rapist. In that moment, as I stood on tiptoes in a most punishing way, I hated myself more than he did. I deserved this.

The turn of a knob ricocheted, ringing through my ears, and a sliver of light beamed toward me an instant before it was extinguished. Impossibly, the blackness became even more suffocating. I heard him coming near, though he barely made a sound.

His touch landed on my shoulder, and I wondered how he found me so easily. His fingers were warm and soft, starkly different from the chill I couldn't escape. My teeth chattered as his caress fluttered across my breasts, and my moan rent the air like a sword, tearing the quiet in two.

Clothing swished, and his arm brushed mine as he moved to stand behind me. His breath hit my ear before his words did. "All those years I was in prison, did you even think of me once?"

Twisting my aching wrists, I shuffled my feet, but my limbs refused to stop quaking. "Please let me down."

"Answer the question."

"I wrote you letters," I blurted, then drew in a quick breath. In the wee hours of the morning when sleep eluded me, I'd bared my soul to him on paper. All the guilt I'd carried, how I felt about him. I'd also laid out every last detail of the secrets I kept locked away.

"I never got any letters."

"I never sent them." Why had I opened my mouth about the letters? If he ever found them…oh God.

"Then why write them?"

"Because I…"

"Spit it out, Alex."

"I missed you."

"You missed me?" He fisted my hair. "You do realize how ridiculous that sounds, right? *You* sent me away."

"I know." I grimaced as his tug on my hair increased.

"What part of me did you miss? The guy you couldn't resist gawking at, or the guy who actually gave a shit about you?"

Past tense. He didn't care about me anymore. I couldn't blame him, but the knowledge hurt something fierce, threatened to chew a hole in my heart. "I just missed you, Rafe."

"Did you write about all the dirty things you wished I'd do to you?"

"No."

"Liar," he murmured into my ear. "Tell me about your

fantasies."

I tried shaking my head, mortified, but his fist in my hair immobilized me.

"If you don't start talking, you're staying down here until morning." His hand dropped, and I sensed him retreating.

"Don't go!" I cried. "I'll tell you."

"I know you will. You haven't changed. I knew eight years ago I could probably do anything I wanted, but I knew better."

"And now?" I asked, hesitance creeping into my tone.

"Now I'm black on the inside. I just don't give a fuck anymore."

"I don't believe that. I still remember who you are, even if you don't."

"Would the man you remember have strung you up on your toes?"

Definitely not.

"Didn't think so," he said, as if he'd heard my thoughts. "So talk. Tell me all of your dirty secrets."

Oh God. The way he breathed those words into my ear was enough to unravel me. "I've thought about you making love to me."

"Do I seem like a making-love kind of guy?"

"No." He seemed like a fuck-you-until-you-split-in-two kind of guy. The kind of guy who'd bring new meaning to the word passionate.

"C'mon, Alex. Last chance to spill before I walk through that door alone."

"I've thought about you going down on me."

He rimmed my earlobe with his tongue, invoking a jittery sigh. "Did you get yourself off thinking about my tongue on your pussy?" He closed a hand around my throat, arched my neck, and darted his tongue inside my ear in an erotic demonstration of what he could do with his hot mouth on other areas of my body.

"You're an ass," I said, though the breathless quality of my voice took the sting out of the words.

"I want to fuck yours."

I couldn't help but tremble. The idea wasn't pleasant, but at the same time, the thought of Rafe sliding inside my tight, forbidden hole...there was something tantalizing about it.

His harsh laughter brought me back to the here and now. "Fuck, you're getting hot thinking about it, aren't you?"

"No." I shook my head, as if the denial alone wasn't good enough, as if he could see me anyway in the darkness.

"I'm calling bullshit. You want me to fuck your ass."

"I've never...done it before." Anal sex was the one area where I was still a virgin, untainted by Zach's brutal obsession. The thought of Rafe penetrating the last place left untouched turned me on in ways I couldn't explain, yet it also terrified me.

"I can be your first." He wedged a finger between my lips. "I bet you've dreamed of my dick in your mouth too. Do you like sucking cock?"

I closed my lips and sucked, unable to stop myself. His finger tasted of salt and something that was undeniably *him*. The way he stroked my tongue made me ache to have something much bigger in my mouth. I'd never wanted it before, had often endured Zach's forceful intrusion while giving it my all just so he'd finish that much faster. But Rafe…putting my mouth on him would be different.

He withdrew his finger and traced a wet path down my throat. "I'm going to release you, and you're going to obey every fucking demand, do you understand me?"

"Yes," I said, biting back a moan.

He set me free from the shackles, and my arms fell to my sides, as if weighed down by cement blocks. Not allowing me a chance to stretch my protesting limbs, he pulled me though the blackness, as if a sudden charge of urgency drove him, and my heart thrummed an erratic beat as he pushed me up the stairs, fingers pressing into hips with a touch that was so *not* gentle. His hands on me, gouging with pain and power, flooded my pussy with heat and dampness. My breaths came rapidly, a wheezing sound more in tune with fear than with want, but wanted him, I did.

We entered the living room, and his hands rose to my waist as his mouth closed over my neck, sucking and nipping as he walked me forward, one step at a time. I dropped my head against his shoulder and moaned, eyelids drooping. Parting my lips, I thought I spoke his name, but if I did, it was lost to our heavy breathing.

He halted at the edge of the room and pulled down a stepladder. "Climb up," he said with a groan. His hard-on jabbed my spine, and his large hands wrapped around my sides as he guided me up the steep passage. He switched on a light, and I saw the top consisted of a loft bedroom with a slanted ceiling. Double skylights undoubtedly gave the illusion of space during the day, though the king size bed took up most of the room. It was cozy and inviting, and I wanted to sink into the mattress and find out if it was as soft as it looked, preferably while his naked body blanketed mine.

He whirled me around, and I met his gaze, plummeting into impossibly green depths shadowed by lashes longer and thicker than mine. Those eyes radiated manic obsession, devouring me with a feverous edge. He pounced without warning, muscles bunching as he hoisted me up by the neck. I kicked my feet helplessly as he strode across the room and slammed me onto the bed. This was about more than sex. He wanted to hurt me—I felt it in my bones where his hands had left their imprints.

Gasping, I propped up on elbows and watched him

warily, my shaking knees falling to the sides. He stalked me slowly, shedding his clothes with each step closer, and his fierce expression said I belonged to him. I shouldn't feel excitement, shouldn't feel warmth pooling between my legs, but that was me—the fucked up girl who got off when she shouldn't.

"Turn over," he growled. "On your hands and knees."

I rolled to my stomach, pushed onto all fours, and the mattress lowered when he climbed behind me. He wrapped his large hands around my hips and dragged me backward until my bottom pressed into his lap, my thighs spread as far as they would go. A rough hand shoved my cheek to the mattress, and my strangled moan tore through the air as his erection teased the opening of my sex.

"Are you on birth control?"

The question evoked a deep ache in my heart. I'd been on some form of contraception since I was fifteen. "I just had an injection a couple of weeks ago."

"Are you clean?"

"Are you?" I countered.

"I've been in prison for eight years. What do you think?"

I didn't answer, as I didn't like to think of Rafe in prison.

"I asked you a question," he bit out in that unnerving tone I was beginning to recognize. "Are you clean?"

I'd only been with one man, and considering Zach's obsession with me, I doubted I had to worry about STDs. I *wished* Zach had turned his focus onto someone else, as horrible and selfish as that sounded. "I'm clean."

He curled his fingers into my hips and nudged me. "Do you want this?"

God yes.

I let out a pleading moan. I shouldn't want him this way. It was twisted and wrong, but just the thought that he'd do it anyway if I fought him made me even hotter. I hated my body; it had it all backwards. Sex shouldn't be about power and control.

His hands closed around my wrists and yanked them to the mattress, next to my spread thighs, and I'd never felt so helpless and exposed—not in a way that was so exhilarating.

"I won't be gentle."

My whole body shuddered. "I don't expect you to be."

"Good, 'cause I'm not stopping." Something ominous laced his words.

"You're going to hurt me, aren't you?" Another shiver went through me, and I couldn't decide if I was exited or horrified. Zach had hurt me so many times that it had become second nature, but Rafe wasn't my psychotic step-brother. Rafe was the guy I'd obsessed over for years, and now he had me pinned down and spread, easy prey, and I worried he was about to figure out just how fucked up I was.

"No orgasms allowed."

I groaned. "You're crazy if you think I can hold back." Every atom in my body zinged with the need for him to fill me.

His fingers flexed around my wrists. "I think you're gonna find a way, unless you really want to test me. I'm not fucking you for your pleasure, sweetheart. I'm fucking you because you're my piece of ass."

That was all I'd ever be to him. A piece of ass, a *thing* he held in contempt for unforgivable sins. Lips trembling, eyes stinging with unshed tears, I tried to swallow the hurt, but this wasn't how I'd imagined our first time.

8. CHOKE

RAFE

I *wasn't* a monster. If I told myself that enough times, maybe I'd believe it.

She swiveled her head and looked at me, dark curls tumbling over her shoulder, and her jade eyes glimmered with unspoken hurt. She still didn't understand that I hungered for her pain, her tears. I smacked her hard on the ass. "Keep your head down."

I slammed into her, and her spine arched under my onslaught of savage greed. My entire body ignited with the sensation of being joined. No latex barrier, just pure skin-to-skin contact. Shit, her pussy was ready for me. Tight, wet, hot. If I weren't so on edge, I'd bury myself in her for hours. Finally, after so many fucking years of wanting this girl, I was inside her. The sense of power intoxicated me, as did the discovery that this was more than just sex. I could deny it all I wanted, but our chemistry didn't lie. There was something irresistible about her. It was true when she was fifteen, when my values kept her safe from me. Now she was even more irresistible because she'd come of age, morphed into a woman I wanted to consume, and I was more than justified in taking her.

Swiveling my hips, I shoved deeper and thrilled at the way her body sheathed my cock like a glove. We slid together in sweat and need, and I pressed my thumbs into her wrists where her pulse galloped in tune to my thrusts. The sounds she made, so guttural they vibrated straight to my dick—fuck they sent me flying. I plunged harder, faster, and squeezed her wrists until my fingers whitened at the knuckles.

"You're hurting me," she said, her voice wafting in the air like a tattered feather.

I yanked her upright and wrapped an arm around her shoulders, one hand clamping her arm to trap her against me. The other gripped her throat, fingers on either side of her neck, forcing her head back. Her spine arched as I pumped.

"You feel that? That's my cock inside you." I drove into her violently, increasing the pace, the pain. I wanted to hurt her, wanted her tears. Each thrust was an angry, unforgiving act of punishment—a way to hide what tortured me deep down; things I'd grappled with for eight years. I craved this girl yet hated her guts, all at the same time.

"Please…" she whimpered.

"Please what? You wanted me to fuck you, and now...I...am." I bit back a grunt and flexed my fingers around her throat.

"Rafe...oh God, Rafe! I'm gonna come," she bit the words out through gritted teeth, and those blessed tears I craved slipped from her eyes.

I licked each salty drop from her cheek and let her shame linger on my tongue. "You're *not* coming," I said, clutching her throat and angling her neck to the side. I sank my teeth into tender, creamy skin and clamped down harder when a screeching cry tore from her lips. My dick celebrated that wail.

"That's right, sweetheart. Cry for me. Fight me."

"Can't…stop…it." Her voice lilted into a continuous moan that wrecked me as her pussy clenched.

She wasn't fighting, wasn't struggling or begging. She was fucking getting *off*.

Oh fuck no. She *would* struggle.

I inhaled deeply, seeking absolute control because anything less was dangerous. It'd been too long since I'd experienced the addictive rush of adrenaline flooding my system, a high I only achieved by stealing someone's breath and sanity, when I was God to them in those seconds when they straddled the line of life and death at my hands.

I couldn't screw this up because no matter what I told her, she meant too much. I wanted her struggle and her terror, but I didn't want to kill her. I tightened my fingers around her throat, adding just enough pressure to restrict the blood flow to her brain.

She writhed like a rabid animal, her fingernails digging into any part of me she could reach. Blood rushed my cock, and I'd never felt so hard, so insane and frantic as I rammed her from behind. Her body bowed backward, and I counted the seconds as I came. She relaxed in my arms as the last bit of pleasure shot from my dick. I withdrew, heart pumping too fast, and laid her limp body onto the mattress.

9. REGRET

ALEX

Strong, muscular arms surrounded me as I gasped, and I clawed at my throat, fighting against the horrifying experience of not being able to breathe. Despite the disorientation and confusion, I sank deeper into his warmth, loving how his body folded around mine. I coughed and gasped some more, and little by little, clarity returned. Cold, harsh reality doused the warm and fuzzies.

Rafe had tried to choke me.

I struggled from his hold and made it to the edge of the bed before he trapped me in his arms again. "Where do you think you're going?"

"You fucking choked me!"

"You fucking came."

"Are you trying to kill me? Do you hate me that much?"

"I don't hate you *that much*, Alex." He moved one arm from my waist and wound a fist in my hair. "You need to remember I'm the one in control here. Just because you have a hot pussy doesn't mean you can disobey me. When I say no orgasms, I mean no orgasms."

Intense hurt welled, unstoppable, and I let out a sob. More followed until I was bawling like a baby. He'd taken something from me—something I'd held onto for years. He'd taken my first time with him, had sullied the memory with his cruelty.

That was something I'd never get back, and it hurt so incredibly bad because he didn't seem fazed. I was just another piece of ass. Even worse, I was someone who deserved his contempt.

I did deserve his hatred, but I didn't deserve to die.

"Stop crying, or I'll put you back in the cellar."

"Why do you have to be such an asshole?"

"Why did you have to send me to prison?" he shot back, adding another painful yank on my hair.

"I didn't want to. God, Rafe…I didn't want to."

"I'm done tiptoeing around this. Either tell me why you did it, or I'll choke you again."

Another sob escaped, and I tried to speak but the words wouldn't come.

He rolled me to my back, pinned both wrists to the mattress with one hand, and circled my throat with the other. My pulse pounded out of control. But he didn't apply pressure. Instead, he stared into my eyes, as if searching for an answer.

"Please…don't. Please…" More tears seeped from my eyes and dripped down the sides of my face. He leaned down and licked them up.

"Either tell me the truth, or you go nighty-night again."

"Please!" I begged. "I didn't want to do it. Rafe…you have no idea."

"Oh, I think I do. That's the interesting thing about being locked up, Alex. I had way too much time to think. You wanted me, only I wasn't giving in, was I?" He lowered his face until we were nose to nose. "You couldn't handle the rejection."

I didn't know if I was more appalled or indignant over his assumptions.

"Admit it! You were nothing but a pampered, spoiled little brat, and you didn't think twice about throwing me away like trash when you didn't get what you wanted."

"I loved you!" I screamed into his face. "I loved you so fucking much." I turned my head and wished the mattress would split open and swallow me.

Oh God. I was ten shades of mortified.

His silence weighed more heavily than his body did.

He flexed his fingers around my locked wrists. "You have a funny way of showing it," he finally said.

I had no answer to that. His hand twitched around my throat, still threatening punishment. "Please, Rafe," I whispered, my voice cracking. "Don't do this."

"Don't do this? You have no idea what *you* did," he said. "I want to squeeze every last breath from you. I want to fucking break you until you're nothing but pieces in my arms."

"Please," I gasped.

"They raped me in there, Alex."

I couldn't breathe, and not because his hands threatened to shut off my air, but for the first time, I really allowed myself to see what I'd done to him. "Kill me," I said, hot, salty drops of regret trickling into my mouth. "I deserve it."

He narrowed his eyes—eyes suddenly bright with pain—and pressed harder on my throat.

My mouth opened, and I gasped as spots floated in the air. The room narrowed, walls closing in a little more with each thump of my heart. I thought it would pound out of my chest. "Do it," I squeaked.

"*Fuck* me," he choked out. The vulnerability in his tone tore me in two. He let go of my throat, and I sucked in air until I thought my lungs would burst.

"I wish I could take it back," I said, squeezing my eyes shut. I'd caused him so much pain, had ruined his life. I'd done this to the only guy I'd ever loved. "I'm sorry. I'm sorry." I said it over and over, wishing he'd believe me, wishing I could turn back time. "If you need to talk about it—"

"Shut up." He returned me to my side and trapped me against his body. "It's late. Get some damn sleep." Instead of returning me to the cellar, he clung to me, one hand fisting my hair while the other claimed my breast. His legs tangled with mine.

I knew this conversation was far from over. He wouldn't stop until he got the truth, and I wondered how long I could hold out. How many choke holds could I handle? How many hours suspended by my wrists, alone in the cold, dank cellar? How many times could I withstand him torturing me with sex?

I brought my fists up, pressed them to trembling lips, and dug sharp fingernails into my palms. When it came to Rafe, I never knew what was coming next, and I didn't know what he was capable of, especially in light of his admission. I shuddered to think of what he'd been through. I *was* a pampered, spoiled brat. Selfish to the core. I should have stopped it. I should have spoken up and told the police the truth, but as the first hours passed, most of them spent in a state of shock, I lost what small bit of courage I might have possessed. Hours turned into days…days into months…months into years.

All the while, Rafe had been in hell.

For all the tough guy front he put up, I believed he did care about me, somewhere inside him where the guy I remembered still existed. He might have loved me, if things had turned out differently. If I hadn't wrecked him.

Life was what it was. I couldn't change the past. I could only deal with the present as it hurtled toward me.

Sometime later, his breathing evened into gentle snores, and I carefully tugged my hair from his fist and lifted his warm palm from my breast. Little by little, I extricated myself from his hold and crawled from bed. When a floorboard creaked under my foot, I froze, fear rising in my throat in the form of a lump. He didn't move. I swallowed hard and inched toward the panel that would drop the ladder onto the first floor.

God, I was quaking like a leaf. The situation reminded me of one of those scary movies I used to make Lucas watch with me—the ones where I'd yell at the heroine, lamenting her stupidity because there was no way she was getting out of there alive.

I had to. For both our sakes. I didn't hold anything against him. The horrors he'd experienced in prison were my fault. I wouldn't take that from him, wouldn't attempt to deflect blame. We all made choices, some good, some bad. When it came to bad decisions, Rafe and I were batting one for one.

So I *had* to get out of there before the situation escalated and he did something we'd both regret.

I kept his sleeping form in my periphery and released the ladder. It dropped to the floor with a ridiculous amount of racket, and my whole body stiffened. He rolled over, underneath the layers of blankets, and for a moment I wanted to crawl back into bed with him. What a ridiculous notion.

As soon as his soft snores resumed, a burst of adrenaline shot through me. I climbed down the steps and landed with a soft thud on the hardwood floor. I turned in the darkened room, thankful for the heavy rain hitting the roof in a cacophony of taps and dings. Under the cover of noise and shadow, I rushed through the house in search of my clothes. Heck, I'd settle for a jacket at this point.

If need be, I'd walk out of that house buck-naked.

I headed toward the kitchen, hoping to find a coat in the closet by the door. Turning the corner, I shook with a mixture of anticipation and dread. It was *deja vu*, and I was back in my house on the night of my engagement, preparing to take hold of freedom with both hands, to hell with the consequences.

I smashed into a body, and at first I thought it was Rafe until the deep voice registered—a voice I didn't recognize.

"What are you doing wandering around by yourself?"

"Rafe!" I screamed, turning and running toward the loft, as if my life depended on it. I screamed for him again as my feet threatened to slide across the hardwood. I was in such a frantic hurry to get up the ladder that my foot slipped on the first rung, and my chin hit the wood hard. I fell on my ass, my jaw throbbing, and palmed my breasts as a figure loomed over me.

10. FLEE

RAFE

Her scream jerked me from sleep, and I sprang to my feet. Adrenaline flooded my system, and I couldn't recall how I got to the opening of the ladder, but I was peering into the darkness when a light switched on. Alex cowered at the bottom, her petite hands covering her tits.

Jax stood next to her. He looked up and took in my questioning glance with a shrug. “She freaked the fuck out, man.”

“Just a sec. I’ll be right down.” I threw on a black shirt, leaving it unbuttoned, and pulled on my jeans. The belt hung over my dick, unbuckled as I descended the steps.

Alex sent me a nervous glance, eyes wide and chest

heaving behind those hands that did little to conceal her tits. Part of me wanted to drag her back to bed and fuck her again. The other part wanted to see how this played out. I already tasted her humiliation, craved it even.

"Get up," I said, my face hardening into a stern expression. I turned toward Jax. "Want a look?"

He arched a brow. "She's a naked woman. What do you think?"

Alex scooted away, bare ass sliding across the hardwood. I grabbed a fist full of her hair and brought her to her feet.

"Leave me alone!" She attempted to pull away, though she still didn't move her hands, and I almost laughed at the way she was standing, like a comical version of a woman needing to pee but trying to hold it.

"Arms at your sides," I ordered. She needed to know I was willing to go to any length to control her, and that included sharing her. Of course, I'd cut off my arm before I'd share her, but she didn't know that. The threat of handing her off to Jax should go a long way toward breaking her stubborn will.

I yanked on her hair. "Hands at your sides!"

Her sob should have cut me to pieces. That would be the normal reaction, but her cries made me want to do dirty, nasty things that would turn those cries into screams. I bunched my hands as she dropped hers. Her nipples puckered, no doubt from the chill in the cabin.

"Touch her tits," I said to Jax.

He narrowed his eyes. "You sure?"

No, not at all. "Yeah, I'm sure."

Alex needed to know she had no sway with me. What better way to show her how little she meant than to let another man fondle her? He reached a hand out, paying no heed to her struggle, and brushed a fingertip across her nipple. Watching him touch her was harder than expected. She sucked in a breath and her body went lax against me, as if she knew she was outnumbered and couldn't stop this.

She was right. She had no control on this island, and it was time she figured it out.

I gritted my teeth as Jax stepped closer and settled both palms over her tits. "You're a lucky man, you sonofbitch."

I might have taken offense, but the name fit my mother perfectly.

"They're a little on the small side, but she's a looker," he said, continuing to mold her tits to his hands.

Agitation twisted her face, and she spit at him. "Get your hands off of me!"

He stepped back, out of the line of spit, and I jerked her back by the hair. "You need to learn a little respect, especially toward my roommate. Jax lives here, so you'd better get used to being naked around him." I grabbed her face, forcing her watery eyes on mine. "If I tell you to let him touch you, you fucking let him touch you. If I tell you to suck his cock, you wrap that sweet mouth around his cock. You're going to do as you're told, got it?"

"No, I don't 'got it,'" she said with a sneer. "I'm not a plaything you can pass around to your buddies. What the hell is wrong with you?"

I raised a brow. "What the hell is wrong with me?" I shoved her to her knees and held her head between hands that shook with rage. "What's wrong with me is your attitude." Fuck, she was getting under my skin. "Jax, unzip." I took in his stunned expression. Obviously, he hadn't expected this development, and neither had I, but it was too late to back down, even if the thought of her mouth touching his cock before it touched mine set my blood boiling.

He only displayed a moment of hesitancy before unbuttoning his jeans. Alex was a tempting package, and I doubted there was a straight man alive that would pass up the chance to have that mouth fastened around his dick. Even Jax, who had issues when it came to being touched, wouldn't say no.

He lowered his zipper and whipped out his junk. She tensed, edging her head sideways as he came near her. I tightened my hold, indecision warring within me. I wanted her mouth around my cock, no one else's, but I needed to see this through.

Jax took another step and stopped just short of

brushing his tip against her lips.

"Open your fucking mouth," I told her.

She jerked her head back and forth, so I pressed my fingers into her jaw until she had no choice but to open. I glanced at Jax. "Give her a taste."

Visibly swallowing, he slowly inched his tip past her lips.

"You like him on your tongue? How about if he really goes for it? Have you ever had a man deep-throat you?"

Her protest came out as a mangled reply around his dick, and her tears slid onto my hands while I forced her head still.

Jax's eyelids fell, and I caught the slight shudder in his body. The tightness of his face wasn't one of pleasure, and I realized this was going too far for him. Fuck, who was I kidding? This was going too far for me.

"You either suck his cock, or you go back into the cellar. Your choice."

She jerked her head back. "Cellar," she said, no hesitation whatsoever, and I smiled. The only cock she wanted was mine. I pulled her to her feet, and Jax stumbled back and zipped his pants.

I pushed her to the door of the cellar, and he followed, though he didn't trail us down the stairs. The door shut with a loud bang. She flung my hands off her and backed up, toward the racks of wine bottles. The tears that trickled down her face, dripping onto her tits, should have softened me, but they didn't. I wanted to lick each one from her skin, savoring the salt on my tongue. Savoring her pain.

The law saw me as nothing more than a rapist. A degenerate. I wouldn't want to disappoint them now.

"Get in the cage."

"No!" She snatched a wine bottle, stared at it for a couple of seconds in her shaking grasp, and busted it on the wall. Deep red wine splashed at her feet. Lifting an unsteady arm, she gripped the jagged neck with whitened knuckles and widened her stance, as if ready to fight me.

Shit, she probably was. Maybe I'd finally found the secret button of hers—the one that sent her into a corner cowering with the realization that a cruel sonofabitch held her life in his hands. No more notions of romance and love-making. But she wasn't exactly cowering now. She was ready to take me on, like a cornered tiger.

Fuck, it was a turn-on, especially since my claws were bigger than hers. "Put it down," I said, the words tearing from my lips in a snarl.

"You're crazy, Rafe! How could you offer me up to him?" she screamed the words, her face distorted into something I'd never seen on her delicate features. "How could you choke me?" Her entire body trembled, and I recognized the adrenaline rushing through her, the need to take control, but I didn't believe she had it in her.

Until she jumped at me with the makeshift weapon

and swiped the air.

Shit. She wasn't kidding.

I put my hands up. "Calm down. At least I wouldn't try to slice you up, sweetheart."

"Stop calling me that!" Her face twisted in despair. "Please, let me go. Please…Rafe. I don't want to hurt you."

"Sweetheart," I said, just to goad her, "you're not even close to hurting me."

She only hesitated an instant before her arm shot out again and jagged glass came way too close for comfort.

Ducking, I caught her wrist and squeezed until the bottle dropped and splintered at our feet. "Come at me like that again and you'll wish the devil was down here with you." I wrenched her hands behind her back, trapped her against me, and wrapped an arm around her throat. Her breaths puffed out, each slow exhale indicating she was giving in. At least, that's what I thought. I loosened my arm, a mistake, because she sank her teeth into my inked bicep, stomped on my foot, and tore up the stairs.

11. PHOBIA

ALEX

Why isn't he grabbing me?

That was my only thought as I ran up the stairs. Each step seemed agonizingly slow, as if I were in a dream, someone on my heels chasing me, and I couldn't get my legs to move fast enough. I pulled the door open and ran smack into a broad chest.

Jax grabbed my shoulders, and his fingers gouged my bones.

"Let me go!" I lifted a knee and aimed for his balls, and when he doubled over with a groan, I took off running. Time seemed to slow, and every footstep felt as if I were forging through mud. I reached the door, flung it open, and lurched into the cold. I didn't dare look back.

They could have been a foot behind me and I wouldn't have known, and I was too scared to find out.

Breaths coming in shallow gasps, I raced over rough ground. Rocks bit into my feet and wind whipped hair into my eyes as rain drenched my body. At this point, I didn't care that I was running naked in the middle of nowhere, exposed to the weather.

A streak of lightening lit up the sky, and I saw a break in the trees.

"Alex!"

My heart pounded in my chest, as loud as the thunder overhead as I recognized the fury in Rafe's voice. He sounded much too close. I buckled down and made for the trees, hoping to find a road on the other side, the source of the highway noise I'd noticed before from inside the kitchen.

"Stop! Alex!"

I broke through the line of Douglas firs in a full out sprint, but it wasn't a road beyond the trees. Lightening lit up the sky again, and for that mere second, I saw the water. Rain pounded the surface, causing a choppy and violent scene. I skidded, my bare feet scraping over pebbles and dirt, and tried to halt forward motion.

I was too late.

With a terrified shriek, I tipped over the edge, my body twisting around as I fell in with a splash. More lightening streaked the heavens, and I saw Rafe's horrified expression. I screamed for him, arms reaching and thrashing as I sank into the freezing depths. Water closed over my face, and the murky void pulled me under.

Pulled me away from him. Away from my only hope of being saved. I sure as hell couldn't save myself. I couldn't even swim.

I fought, kicked, prayed to reach the surface, and blindly grasped for something to cling to. My lungs burned with the need to breathe. Oh God, it was unbearable. Body going limp, I finally gave up the battle, accepting imminent death. Maybe I deserved it. Maybe it was better this way. At least I'd get the chance to see Mom again, get a chance to explain, to beg her forgiveness.

I thought of Rafe as I opened my mouth and allowed the water to fill my lungs. A sense of peace cocooned me, and I said goodbye to him, told him I loved him. As everything faded to black, I felt hands grabbing me. My body moved swiftly upward, then…nothing.

"Fucking breathe, Alex!"

Someone pounded on my chest.

"Shit, man. I'm so sorry. I shouldn't have let her get away."

"Breathe!"

The voices were strained, as if coming from constricted throats. Cold, wet drops fell on my face, and at first I thought they were tears, but tears were hot and salty, and these drops were like icy pinpricks on my cheeks. Something loud rumbled overhead, blocking out the voices, and the ground vibrated. I felt soft, surprisingly warm lips on mine, opening my mouth and breathing life into me. I came to with a violent cough that seized my body.

"That's it, cough it up." Cold fingers turned my head to the side, and a flood of water erupted from my mouth. I opened my eyes and found Rafe perched over me, his arms supporting his weight and his face inches from mine. "You scared the fucking shit out of me!" he screamed. Water dripped from his hair, down his nose and off his chin.

And his eyes...they narrowed to furious slits. He jumped to his feet and reached out a hand. "Get up," he said between tight lips.

I let him pull me up, and my body quaked uncontrollably. I was still trying to calm down from almost drowning, but as soon as another streak of lightening shot across the sky, the situation hit me head-on.

Too much water.

All around me.

My heart pounded in my ears, galloping at an unbearable speed as panic took over. A keening cry tore from my lips, and I doubled over, hugging my midsection as the world around me tilted. "Why?" That single word squeezed from my throat. "Why would you bring me here?"

"Why do you think?" Shaking his head, Rafe glanced at Jax, who stood off to the side observing the drama unfolding between Rafe and me. "I knew you couldn't escape, but I never thought you'd run and almost get yourself killed!"

I decided not to point out the fact that any sane person would try to run. "Where are we? What is this place?"

"Mason Island." He swept the area with a hand. "But since you're so set on leaving, there's a boat at the dock. Feel free."

"You know I can't!"

"Don't I know it," he said with a sinister laugh. "Why do you think I brought you here?" He pushed me back enough so his eyes bored into mine. "You'll fucking do as I say because there's nowhere for you to go. We both know you won't come anywhere near this water again."

"I hate you!" I screamed, pounding on his chest.

He easily deflected the blows. "Not nearly as much as I hate you. Now move your ass." He pulled me away from the river, toward the cabin, I assumed. I stumbled along numbly, eyes on the ground, one foot in front of the other, and never quite registered anything around me. I could only think of one thing.

Water. Too much water.

He hadn't needed to lock me up. My fear held me prisoner more effectively than any conventional method he could have used. The chains, the shackles, the cage—they'd all been props to mess with my head. As I followed him back toward the cabin, something inside me finally broke. My fear of water stemmed from a near-drowning experience when I was four, and I'd never learned to swim.

Rafe had known. He'd been the one to fish me out of my family's pool when I was fourteen, after Zach "accidentally" knocked me in. My brother had been particularly mean that day, probably because Rafe had stopped by, and I hadn't been able to keep my eyes off him.

How ironic that my phobia was his most powerful weapon.

The three of us entered the cabin through the door off the kitchen, and Rafe switched on a light. Unable to stop shivering, I wrapped my arms around myself and clenched my jaw to stop my teeth from clanking together.

Rafe shrugged out of his soaked black shirt, flung it over a chair, and moved it away from the table. "Jax, take a seat over there, would ya?"

Jax gave him a funny look but followed the request.

"No, I need you to turn the chair around, so the back faces the table."

"Sure thing." Jax turned the chair and plopped onto it

before removing his own wet T-shirt.

My gaze traveled between them, back and forth, and I felt as if I were missing something. I'd just tried to escape. I'd almost drowned, and they were acting nonchalant. Too nonchalant. What the hell was going on here?

Rafe's gaze fell on me, and for a few heavy moments, I didn't breathe. That look, his lips thin, eyes narrowed, made my pulse rocket. A clap of thunder sounded, and I jumped.

Rafe pulled the belt from his pants.

I backed up. "What are you doing?"

He didn't give me a chance to retreat. With a yank on my arm, he brought me closer and wound the belt around my wrists.

"Rafe...please—"

He pulled the leather tight, and I gasped as he bent me over the table with a hard shove. Drops of water landed on the wood, and my breasts flattened against the surface.

He pushed my arms across the table and tossed the other end of the belt at Jax. "Knot it around the chair."

"Rafe?" My voice came out unusually high-pitched, and I swiveled my head in time to see him take down the paddle he'd pointed out earlier that morning. "You wouldn't."

Jax snickered as he attached the belt around a slot in the chair. I pulled on it, but it wouldn't give.

"I definitely would." Rafe brought my attention back to him. His voice chilled me, sending dread and remorse through my blood. Dread for what was coming, and remorse for my actions. I should have been smarter about trying to escape. I should have taken a few days to gain his trust first. This attempt had turned into a disaster.

"My old man only used this on my brother and me a handful of times. It hurt like hell, and you can bet your ass we learned quick. You're about to learn quick too."

I stiffened as he halted behind me. Waiting for that first strike was the worst part, and when he finally did crack that paddle across my ass, I lost my breath for what seemed like forever, though it must have only been a mere instant before he did it again. I jumped from foot to foot and bit into my lip to keep from yowling. I wouldn't give him the satisfaction of voicing my pain.

And I never, ever wanted him to know how this was turning me on. My face burned from humiliation—not from what he was doing, but rather from my own sick reaction to it.

"C'mon, sweetheart, scream for me. Beg me to stop."

"No," I ground out through gritted teeth.

He struck again, and this time I let out an involuntary yelp.

"That's better."

Crack!

"Stop!" I clenched my thighs, and my hands fisted

within the restraint of the belt. Jax caught my gaze, and I noticed his fingers curling around the chair back, knuckles turning ash-white. He licked his lips, eyes glazed over with arousal.

Rafe continued to paddle my ass, and the three of us fell into an odd sort of silence. There was no talking, and I held back any sounds of pain, or God forbid, pleasure. Only the smack of thick wood to skin echoed through the room.

I drifted into a space outside myself as Rafe increased the pressure of the strikes. After about thirty, he set the paddle down on the table, his breathing coming fast and hard. I sensed him moving closer, heard a zipper lower, and I tightened my already clenched muscles.

"Spread your legs."

Hands forming fists, I let my head drop to the table as I parted my thighs. Mortification burned my cheeks again, hotter than before because he was about to fuck me in front of his friend. Even worse, they were about to learn the truth about me.

His hands fell to my hips, and he entered me with a single, forceful plunge. "Fuck, you're wet." He laughed, thrusting so hard, he pushed me higher onto the table until my feet left the floor. "I would've never guessed. You get off on this shit, don't you?"

A tear leaked out, and I squeezed my eyes shut. "I'm sorry," I said with a moan.

"Are you apologizing because you get off on pain and humiliation, or are you apologizing for something else?"

"I'm just...sorry." Sorry for being the way I was because my fucked up nature was at the root of why he'd gone to prison. I was sorry for so much.

He slowed the pace, his cock sliding in and out with gentle rhythm. I scratched my nails on the surface of the table and moaned.

Jax let out a moan too. I lifted my head as he reached for his zipper. His head fell back, hooded eyes watching me as his hand pumped in his lap.

Rafe's shallow thrusts tormented me, rubbing in just the right spot. My need dripped down my thighs, seeping from my body in a gentle pull that made me grind my teeth. I abused the air with deep, throaty cries.

"I need to come," I begged.

"No, you're not getting off. If you do, I'll choke you again."

I gasped. "I can't hold back!"

"I said no." He smacked my ass and rammed me. Hard. Painfully hard. I concentrated on anything but him moving inside me. The thunder reverberating overhead, the hard edge of the table biting into my belly, the eerie howl of a train. Even Jax's grunts as he neared orgasm. Anything but Rafe.

It wasn't enough. I was going to come again, and he was going to choke me, a thought that terrified me. I could handle a lot of things, but having my air cut off wasn't one of them. Unbidden, the image of Zach entered my mind, and I held onto it, remembered all the times he'd dragged my panties down and pinned me to the bed. My bed. The one place I was supposed to feel safest. I recalled how he'd muffled my sobs in the pillow, how he'd beaten me in places where the bruises wouldn't show. Still, my body had turned on me.

This was his fault. He'd made me the way I was, and I hated him for it.

Rafe pushed into me one last time and stilled, fisting my hair as he came. Jax came too, as if they'd timed it. His breathing gradually slowed as he traced a lazy path down my back. Gooseflesh erupted from his touch—a sensation that contrasted with the searing ache in my core. He released my hands, picked me up, and threw my soaked body over his shoulder like a sack of potatoes. Water dripped from my hair and left a trail on the floor as he carried me toward the cellar. He stopped on the way and grabbed a towel from the bathroom.

I was shivering violently when he approached the cage. "Don't leave me in there. Please." I clutched his wet jeans, but he dislodged me way too easily and set me on my feet.

"Two nights, Alex. That's what your little escape attempt earned you." He kept me at his side, one hand fisting my hair as he unlocked the cage. He shoved me inside, and the towel landed on the concrete at my feet.

I turned around and helplessly watched while he shut and secured the door. "Rafe…please…" I blinked several times, but his unwavering expression swam in my vision.

"Do I need to restrain your hands?"

"Why would you need to do that?" I gestured to my prison. "It's not like I'm going anywhere."

He laughed. "No masturbating."

The idea of touching myself was the last thing on my mind. In fact, I was pretty certain if I did, it would only make me want the real thing more. I still ached for him, so much, despite the wall of bars standing between us while he held the key to my freedom.

"I'll be back in the morning to feed you." He turned, as if I meant nothing, and once again the darkness suffocated me.

12. TURNING POINT

RAFE

Two things haunted me: I had a son I'd yet to meet, and I had a naked captive in the cellar—a tempting, kinky one I ached to fuck again. I adjusted my jeans and tried to force my mind onto other things, but the fact that two days had gone by, in which I hadn't dealt with either issue, wouldn't leave me alone.

Neither would Nikki. She'd tried calling several times —I had eight unheard messages on my cell but was too chicken-shit to listen to them, let alone return her calls. I had no clue what to say to her anyway, mainly because she had no clue I'd kidnapped a woman and was now holding said woman in my cellar. Those weren't exactly the actions of father material. The kid was probably better off never knowing me.

The cabin was too fucking quiet, too still. Alex had remained unnervingly silent, even when I'd gone down there to feed her, and Jax had gone into work. Enough was enough. She was mine—mine to play with, mine to torment. Fucking *mine.* If I wanted to fuck her again, I would. No more thoughts of how terrified she'd looked when she'd fallen into the river, or how my heart stopped as I tried to get hers working again.

My footsteps fell heavily on the stairs, and when I reached the bottom, I found her huddled in her favorite corner, her cheek to the concrete and body curled into a ball underneath the towel I'd left with her. It was cruel and inhumane, but damn, it was a sight I'd never forget. Besides, better to be hard and mean now, get her to fall into line, than return her to the cellar numerous times because I'd been too soft on her. I definitely didn't want a repeat of the river.

Something enfolded my heart and squeezed. Fuck, she'd almost died, and whether I liked it or not, part of me would have died with her. My actions had nearly gotten her killed, and regardless of what she'd done, I couldn't live with myself if anything happened to her. I wanted to punish her, but I also couldn't deny that I straight up wanted her. *Period.*

She'd become my world, my obsession, and I had no plans to let her off this island.

"If I let you out, will you behave?"

"Yes," she said, the word falling from her lips in lifeless fashion. Maybe I'd finally broken her.

"Will you try to run again?"

"You know I won't. Where would I go?"

"Things are going to change around here. No more tantrums, no more back-talking or throwing dishes." I paused long enough to unlock the cage and enter. "No more escape attempts. You'll do as you're told, when you're told, without argument, or next time you'll spend a lot more time down here. Do you understand me?"

"Y…yes," she said through chattering teeth. "I'm so cold."

Damn it. I was walking a fine line between breaking her and risking her becoming ill. "Okay." Crouching, I brushed tangled hair from her eyes. A strand caught between her lips, and I ran a finger along the seam of her mouth to remove it. Her lips were chapped, her face pale, but what bothered me most was the emptiness in her expression. I remembered how deep her fear of water ran, and I shuddered as images flashed in my mind. Her eyes wide with terror, arms reaching for me as she splashed into the murky river.

Shaking off the recollections, I pulled her to her feet, then stood back and gave her time to stretch her muscles. "C'mon," I said, reaching out a hand. "Let's get you clean and warm, then you can start that good behavior by making dinner." We made our way up to my bedroom, where I directed her into the bathroom. Her eyes grew large and round at the sight of the garden tub.

"Alex, the shower." I pointed to the huge stall tucked on the other side of the tub. Last thing I needed was an episode of hysterics.

She folded her arms. "You don't have to stay. I can shower on my own. There's nowhere for me to—" She cut off when she turned to face me. Her gaze followed my movements as I lifted the hem of my T-shirt up my chest, and I couldn't help the smirk that flitted across my lips.

"No, sweetheart. I'm getting in with you." I gestured toward the stall, a large enclosure of walls made with blue and grey tile. A narrow opening served as the entrance. She gawked at me a for a few seconds, and I was so close to shoving her inside because shit…I couldn't wait to get my hands on her body.

13. SHOWER HEAD

ALEX

My mouth gaped at his muscular chest, and I couldn't tear my eyes from him when he lowered his jeans. The charcoal gray boxer briefs went the way of his pants. He displayed his body without shame or modesty. I took in every inch of him, especially the dark tribal lines that streaked across the left side of his chest and down both arms. I wanted to follow that map with my lips and fingertips, wanted to lick down his muscles, past his abs, only stopping long enough to tease his erection with my tongue.

"Have you seen enough yet?"

I jumped, lifting my attention to his face, and felt my own flush. Furious Rafe scared the shit out of me, and naked, lustful-looking Rafe made me just as nervous. Both versions were passionate and cold, stable one minute yet irrational the next. I lowered my gaze to his erection. Moisture collected at the tip, and some secret part of my psyche celebrated. I did that to him, without even touching him.

He couldn't hide his desire like I could mine, collecting between my closed thighs, stowed away and out of sight.

This was the first time I'd felt anything during the past two days. While locked away in the dark, I'd found a way to shut down. Maybe I'd experienced a delayed reaction to the horror of nearly drowning, but when he left me alone in that cellar, shivering more violently than ever before, my brain simply stopped functioning like normal. Somehow, I'd found a way to cope.

I'd pretended to be somewhere else. Someone else. I'd made up a new identity. In my new dream world, I called myself Amy. Amy was plain and boring and absurdly *happy*. Amy had a loving, devoted husband, two adorable kids, and a perfect, non-smelly dog named Zippo. Amy lived in the south, possibly Arizona, where it was dry and sweltering under the sun.

"Get in," Rafe said, bunching his hands, and the fantasy of another life dissolved, leaving cold, hard truth in its wake.

I resisted the urge to cover myself as I entered the

shower. Next to his beautiful physique, my filthy and unkempt body with curves in all the wrong places paled in comparison.

He stepped in after me and turned on the dual shower heads. Hot spray filled every corner, hitting us from all directions. I gasped when he shoved me against the freezing tile. Without a word, he grabbed a bottle of shampoo and squirted some into a palm before rubbing both hands together.

I closed my eyes and focused on breathing as he started washing my hair, but when he added more soap and slid his hands down my shoulders and over my breasts, I almost came undone, unprepared for those hands gliding over me. As his fingers blazed along my skin, I wrestled with my demons, the ones that lived to remind me of what a dirty whore I was. I'd never experienced what was considered a normal physical reaction to sex, the ability to enjoy it without the threat of force or violence. No one had ever made me feel like this. Rafe had more power in a single touch than Zach had in his entire being.

The heat flaming between my thighs was undeniable, unbearable, and I whimpered when those strong hands drifted over my stomach and smoothed down my legs.

"I'll have to buy you a shaving kit." He caressed behind a knee. "I want to shave these legs."

A shiver traveled along my skin from head to toe,

contradictory to the hot shower. He worked his way up my body and tilted my head so the water sluiced over my face and hair.

"Soap's gone. You can open your eyes now." His gaze transfixed me, capturing me in green depths from which I'd never return. "Raise your arms."

Later, I might question why I did it without hesitation. I brought my arms up and held them high. I didn't think about disobeying, especially when he dropped to his knees and licked his lips, his gaze on my pussy.

"Spread your legs."

Holy hell. Sucking in a breath, I widened my stance. He wrapped his arms around my hips, hands clutching my ass, and pulled my pelvis toward his face. But he didn't put his mouth on me. Not yet. He took his time, languid gaze roaming past belly and breasts before settling on my face.

The sight of Rafe naked and on his knees, dark hair plastered to his forehead and drops of water hanging on his lashes, was the most gorgeous view in existence. Reality was far better than the dream.

Except for the part where he'd kidnapped me.

"What do you want from me?" I whispered, confused because he was being so gentle. He'd shown me nothing but cruel detachment since he'd taken me…until I'd fallen into the river.

A violent tremor raced through me, and that night

came rushing back; the freezing water closing over my head, the realization I was going to die. Something else broke through the fog that had blanketed me for the past couple of days. Him. The way he'd reacted, how he'd been furious and punishing but also fearful of losing me.

It dawned on me that my almost drowning had rattled him, and I wondered what it meant.

His gaze held mine, unblinking as water streamed down his face. "I want many things from you, but right now I want to taste you." He leaned forward, and I thought I'd pass out when his tongue slid between my folds.

"Oh God, Rafe."

His fingers dug into my ass, and he let out a long groan that vibrated straight to my core. I balled my hands, struggling to keep them raised, and let my head fall back against the tile. My body sang for him, quivered and ached with the mere brush of his lips, the teasing scrape of teeth. My breaths burst out in short gasps, and I closed my eyes and let the water wash over my forehead and cheeks as an orgasm built. I was so close. Two more strokes of his tongue, and my toes would curl. I'd slide to the floor in completion, limbs as fluid as the water beating down on us.

He jerked back and looked up at me, a hard glint in his eyes.

"Don't stop." I thrust my hips toward him, a silent

plea for him to finish. He rose and held my face, mouth hovering an inch from mine as our eyes locked, and licked the water from his lips.

My jaw slackened, and I felt the spray from the shower misting on my tongue. He was going to kiss me. I was sure of it. "Rafe," I whispered, aching to taste him. Just once.

He pulled my arms down. "Wrap your hand around me."

I closed my fingers around his erection, and my palm glided over silky smooth skin. His breath shuddered out with every stroke and mingled with mine in a frenzy of want and need. The air between us grew moist and warm from the steam of the shower.

"Fuck," he groaned, his forehead falling against mine, "that feels incredible. Keep going."

Mindlessly, I rubbed him and watched in wonder as he lost himself to my touch. With each groan and sigh that erupted from his beautiful mouth, my own need bloomed out of control.

"I want you so much," I said.

He let out a growl and stilled my movement. "You're not getting off."

If he intended to drive me mad by using my desire for him as a weapon, then he'd have no problem succeeding.

Rafe had turned into a cruel son of a bitch.

"Get on your knees, sweetheart." How I hated that

endearment coming from his lips. He said it with scorn, made it sound like an insult. Hands gripping my shoulders, he pushed down hard until my knees buckled.

The thought of sucking his cock shouldn't excite me so much. Shit, I was in big trouble. He was toying with me, making me hot and wet for him, and leaving me with no end in sight.

He angled my head back, his touch somehow gentle despite the iron-like hold he had on me. I opened my mouth, my heart thudding in my ears as he pushed his cock inside.

"Fuck. I haven't had a woman suck me off in eight years."

His admission filled me with a sense of power. I'd be the one to bring him pleasure after all this time. I closed my lips around his shaft and peeked up at him, needing the connection, but he avoided eye contact. He tipped forward, palms slamming against the tile, and his chest rose and fell shallowly, biceps rippling, tattoos a dark sheen underneath the water.

He grunted with each thrust, and his essence infused my tongue with the heady taste of him. I wanted him inside me so badly—a desperate need I was certain would destroy me.

You're not getting off.

Eventually, he was going to fuck me again.

And eventually, I was going to break from frustration.

14. SHOWTIME

RAFE

Holy shit. Her mouth was heaven. Hot, almost too damn hot, and tight around my dick. She took her time with the tip, rolling her tongue in circular motions before licking down the underside. My head dropped against the tile, and my mind shattered, thoughts lost to the roar of the water. I couldn't look at her, didn't want her to see how completely unglued I was.

This spitfire of a woman, a woman I had every reason to hate, made me question everything.

Damn, it'd been too fucking long since I'd had a woman on her knees pleasuring me. I tried convincing myself that was the only reason for the intensity in my groin, that it had nothing to do with *who* was sucking my cock, but that didn't fly. I thrust my hips forward, needing to go deeper. Faster.

She edged back and made a gagging noise, but I shoved my hands into her wet, tangled hair and growled. No way in hell was I letting her pull away. She was going to swallow my load, every last bit of it. I expected her to fight me, but instead she did something that stunned the hell out of me; she fondled my balls in her warm palm and moaned. Fuck, Alex getting off on sucking my cock was fucking amazing.

I glanced down and found her gaze trained on me as her lips slid along my shaft. Hot damn…she was good at this. The sexiest thing about her eyes was the genuine need in them. She wasn't putting on a show or giving me a fake sultry stare like other women used to. She took me deep in her throat and gagged, but she didn't retreat.

"Alex…" I hissed in a breath between clenched teeth. "That. Keep doing *that*. Almost there."

She gagged again, and that was my undoing. Thank God for small favors. I curled my fingers in her strands, holding her immobile, and pushed deeper. I wanted as deep as possible—wanted her helpless because up until then, she'd held all the power.

My mind disconnected, floating where only liberation existed, and I ground my eyes shut, groaning as my release spurted down her throat.

She finished swallowing, and reluctantly, I let her pull

those amazing lips from my shaft. Her needy expression was almost too much, and when she placed a tender kiss on the tip of my cock, something inside me wanted to crack. I almost did. She was bringing me back from the brink, bit by bit, and only the reminder of the hell she'd put me through kept me on course.

She whispered my name, a question in her tone.

"Quiet," I said, not ungently, but I seriously needed a few seconds to collect myself. Damn it, my dick was still hard. I hated that I didn't have a handle on my control, but I guessed that was to be expected after going so long without sex, and fucking her twice wasn't enough. I suspected it would never be enough with her.

I was *this* close to taking her to bed, and if I had my way, we wouldn't leave it for at least three days.

I couldn't do that. Giving her exactly what she wanted, which ironically was me, wasn't what I intended to do. Maybe someday, after she came clean with the truth, we could really work past our problems and find a fucked up version of normal.

Our normal.

I didn't see that happening for a while. Too much of me still hated her…but too much of me still wanted her. How more messed up could I get?

I shut off the water, stepped from the shower, and grabbed two towels before handing her one.

She wrapped her body in soft green terrycloth. "Can I

please have my clothes back now?"

"No way." I ran my gaze up and down her body, taking in her long legs, the gentle swell of cleavage, and the curve of her waist. Even obscured by the towel, she was the definition of fuckable. "I like knowing you're naked and accessible at all times. If I tell you to bend over so I can fuck you, I don't want clothing in the way."

She wouldn't look at me as she finished drying her skin, then, with her lower lip caught between her teeth, she slowly let the towel drop. "I'm ready."

Somehow, I guessed there was a double meaning to those words. I'd bet the deed to this island she was still wet and throbbing for me, which was how I wanted her. In fact, I wanted her in a constant state of arousal. My cock twitched at the thought. Playing this game with her could be more fun than I imagined.

I quickly dressed and led her down the ladder and into the kitchen. Grabbing a beer from the fridge, I settled at the table and popped the cap. "Start dinner."

She seemed lost at first, her gaze veering in my direction every so often as she perused the kitchen. I wondered if she even knew how to cook, considering her spoiled upbringing included an on-demand chef and a housekeeper. I didn't feel obliged to give her any pointers. I rather enjoyed watching her flounder. If she wanted to stay out of trouble, she'd figure out how to make something edible. After five minutes of opening and closing the cupboard doors, followed by the fridge and freezer, she settled on baking chicken.

She bent over, her perfect ass aiming straight at me, as she slid the pan into the oven, and by the time she shut the door, I had a raging hard-on again. My body wanted her constantly, and I couldn't stop myself from grabbing her, mid-stride, and settling her on my lap. I pushed her legs apart until she straddled me, and she had to realize exactly what I needed from her. Wrapping a hand around the back of her neck, I drew her close, aching to taste her lips, but I stopped before we connected.

Kissing was intimate. Kissing usually fucked everything up by bringing feelings into the mix. But hell, she smelled amazing—a mixture of soap and something that was one hundred percent Alex.

Her stomach rumbled, reminding me that she was supposed to be finishing dinner, not sitting on my lap, tempting me to fuck her or do something as asinine as *kiss* her.

"You're driving me crazy," she said, head falling back and eyes drifting shut. A frustrated sigh escaped her lips.

She was driving *me* crazy. I grabbed her hips and pulled her snug against my cock, and the only thing keeping me from fucking her was my own damn clothing. Maybe we should both walk around naked. I rubbed against her, and the rough texture of my jeans created friction on her clit.

She moaned, her head falling to my shoulder, tits smashing against my chest as she clung to me. "I can't take much more of this."

"If you tell me why you lied, I'll make you come so fucking hard, you'll forget your own name."

With a shudder, she tangled her hands in my hair, fingers clutching in desperation. "You're evil," she groaned. If her touch didn't feel so good, I would have trapped her hands behind her back.

"Tell me, sweetheart," I said, my lips brushing her ear. "Tell me what I want to know, and I'll put you out of your misery." I gripped her nape and scraped my teeth across her throat. "But if you keep up this bullshit, you're gonna learn what the female equivalent of blue balls is." I rubbed against her again to make my point. She trembled in my arms, and I felt the dampness from her pussy seeping through my jeans.

"You were right the other night," she said. "I was young and selfish. I couldn't handle you rejecting me."

Now that she'd said the words, they didn't ring true. I'd known she had a thing for me, but would she really sink so low as to ruin my life because I wouldn't touch jailbait? I wasn't sure why I hadn't considered it before, but something else was going on...something she was hiding. I pushed her to her feet, gave her a dark smile when she pulled that lower lip between her teeth, and reached for the button on my pants. Her gaze settled on my lap and never strayed as I inched down my zipper. I freed my cock, grabbed her hips and twirled her around, and pulled her onto my shaft.

She was so fucking wet.

Wrapping both arms around her, I brought a hand up and circled her throat. Our bodies slapped together in a crazy rhythm that tilted me closer to the edge with each thrust.

"You're lying to me."

"I'm not," she bit out with a groan, and it was such a torturous sound one would think I was beating the shit out of her instead of fucking her.

I flexed my fingers. "Tell me the truth and I'll let you come."

She remained silent, and I wasn't sure if she flat-out refused to talk, or if she was scared to. Either way, I'd find out the truth, and I wouldn't stop pushing until she told me. I nibbled her neck, eliciting a moan from deep in her throat. I increased the pressure of my hand and held her to me when she started thrashing.

I needed this, needed those few heightened seconds as she fought for survival while I spilled into her. I was doing just that, her body going limp in my arms, when Jax walked through the door. "Damn, man. You didn't tell me tonight was dinner and a show night."

15. MORNING GLORY

ALEX

I slept in Rafe's bed, and for the first time since he'd kidnapped me a week ago, I actually slept. Really slept. Most surprising was how he liked to cuddle. I remembered the way he held on to me the night I tried to escape, but I thought he'd done it to keep me from taking off.

Now that he knew I had no intention of leaving the cabin, the way he held my body all night—one palm on my breast while the other wedged between my thighs—I realized this was how he liked to sleep. But what I found even more surprising was how I got any sleep at all, considering the placement of his hands.

So was the way in which I awoke, with his fist

clamping around both wrists and his erection pushing into my mouth.

I opened my eyes and found him straddling my chest, dark hair tumbling onto his forehead as he gazed at me. Well-defined muscles rippled underneath black lines of ink. His body was a masterpiece, God's finest art, and those green eyes…I'd never tire of losing myself in them. I hadn't outgrown him at all, not during the last eight years, not even now that he'd kidnapped me and revealed the darkness festering inside him.

Part of me craved his sinful obsidian desires.

He pulled out and plunged back in, and I rolled my tongue around the tip, tasting the musky salt that signified his need. He braced himself upright, one hand on the headboard, and pushed deeper. I loved how smooth and solid he was in my mouth. I always gagged while giving head, but I wanted to take him all the way in, deep in my throat, and I didn't give a shit if I gagged or not.

He stilled with a shudder, and his lids drooped, though his eyes never left mine, never stopped giving off their hypnotic vibe. "Do you like sucking me off?"

His husky voice doused my skin in a blissful chill, and I tingled all over, tightening my lips around the base of his cock.

"Fuck, Alex, you've got the hottest damn mouth." He started moving again, a slow, torturous pace—torturous because the longer he took, the more I wanted him filling someplace else.

"You're fucking gorgeous, curls everywhere, those lips wrapped around my dick." He tightened his hold on my wrists. "I could get used to waking you up like this."

Oh God, so could I, if he'd only let me come. I clenched my thighs together, but it did nothing to relieve the ache that had throbbed since last night, since he'd choked me into unconsciousness.

He increased the pace, and the taste of him intensified, as did the pressure on my wrists when he edged back and pinched my nose. I flailed in a panic, legs kicking, and tried to pull free of his erection, but he shoved it down my throat and smothered me.

Our gazes crashed together, and my pulse pounded in my temples, ticking away the seconds.

"Trust me, I won't kill you, but I can do this all day. Thirty more seconds, and your lungs will ignite. Blink twice if you're ready to tell me what you're hiding."

I didn't flutter an eyelash. Thing was, I did trust him. He wouldn't kill me. He wouldn't. My body was fast forgetting that though as I struggled for air, as my lungs burned for it.

He pulled out, and I sucked in a gasping breath before he pushed in again, deep down. "How long do you wanna play this game?"

I told myself not to panic and resorted to using the only weapon I had—my mouth. I added suction and swirled my tongue, flicked and darted until his hips thrust in abandon. I couldn't breathe, but I didn't care because I was about to send him over the edge, I could already tell.

"*Fuck*," he said with a growl as he came. He let go of my nose, and I almost choked as he spilled down my throat. He yanked out, and some of his cum spurted onto my lips and chin. "You play dirty."

"Not nearly as dirty as you!" I said, still gasping for air.

His lips quirked up in a lopsided grin. "You have no idea." He curled my fingers around the bars of the headboard before sliding down my body. "Spread your legs."

"No!"

"Spread your *fucking* legs."

Something about his tone made me tremble. I opened my thighs without another word of protest, and he slid his hands underneath my ass, thumbs skimming the entrance of my sex. His mouth parted, hot breath igniting me, and I arch into his erotic kiss with a moan, fingers squeezing the shit out of the bars as his tongue burrowed into me.

My legs fell to the sides, quaking uncontrollably. I gritted my teeth as my center coiled, seconds away from coming undone when he switched to light, closed-mouthed kisses that torturously teased. I held my breath, refusing to cry out in frustration. I needed to come, so bad, and I was seconds away from begging him for it, from grabbing at his skin as if it were my lifeline.

I wanted him all over me, inside me, and wrapping me in his raw and brutal strength.

"Please, Rafe—"

He closed his lips over my clit, and I bowed over the mattress with a wail. He flicked his tongue, just light enough to drive me insane. "Rafe, please…for the love of God, I need more." The headboard shook under the force of my grip.

"So do I," he said, words vibrating along my pussy. "I need the truth." He worked his way to my core, tongue lapping up moisture, before returning to my downfall—that little spot that was an instant away from sending me hurtling into ecstasy-like chaos. Pushing a finger into me, his tongue pressed on my clit hard.

"Oh God…oh my fucking *God*…

He pulled away, and an anguished cry tore from my throat. He propped his head on a hand and looked at me between shamelessly spread legs, my knees bent on either side of him and feet flat on the mattress.

"How bad do you want it?"

"Stupid question."

"Wrong answer." He kissed my hip, then dragged his lips up my stomach before sucking a nipple into his mouth. He slid a palm between my legs and stoked the blaze raging inside me. I thrust my pelvis into his touch, arched my spine, and was about to shatter when he stopped again. My breath expelled in a rush. I hated and loved him all at once, and my body was on the same page.

He brought his hands to my neck and clamped down, and I knew without a doubt he was going to choke me again. I prepared my useless fists to pound against his steel body.

"Fight me, sweetheart."

I stiffened at his demand and refused to move. Part of me wanted to rebel, wanted to gain the upper hand even as he threatened to stifle me.

With a growl, he increased the pressure until I opened my mouth under his crushing weight.

"You're gonna put up a fight, whether you want to or not."

Bastard.

The compression on my neck became unbearable, and the need to break free kicked in. I beat on his chest, shoved against his arms, and made it to my knees, a move he must have allowed because he was too strong for me. My face screamed for relief as I used all the force I had, but I still couldn't get his hands off my throat. We fell to the floor, and I landed hard on my back. He pinned me down, forced my legs apart, and settled his erection at my entrance.

"You want my cock?"

I gasped, more concerned with breathing than with

fucking. "Rafe…stop…" I clawed at his fingers, desperate to get free. His gaze never left mine, and I realized this was how he got off. He craved my helplessness, perhaps because my actions had rendered him helpless for so long.

Or maybe because Rafe "The Choker" Mason got his kicks in holding the lives of others in his hands.

"You're hurting me." Tears leaked out and burned tracks down my cheeks.

He pushed into me violently. "Fuck," he groaned. "Your refusal to tell me the truth is hurting you." His hands pressed harder on my throat.

My body reacted instinctively, and I kicked and squirmed, my useless fingers gouging his. "Please," I squeaked, but the fucked up part was how I was getting wetter with each thrust, despite him choking me. The edges of the room grew dark, and I felt weightless as I drifted into nothingness.

His erratic breathing washed over me as my lids fluttered open. I gripped my throat, wheezing air into burning lungs. He was still pumping, and I was on the verge of coming, even after losing consciousness, when Jax dropped the ladder and popped his head through the opening.

"Dude. Someone just showed up."

16. VISITOR

RAFE

Too many thoughts battled in my head. The possibilities were endless and in each one, someone discovered Alex. A cop. Nikki. Even Zach. I didn't like unexpected developments. Since her declared death had hit the news, I'd grown lax.

My mistake.

I pulled out of her and wound an arm around her neck, smothering her mouth with my hand. "Who is it? Did you let them in?"

Jax shook his head. "It's a woman. I have no idea who she is or what she wants."

"Grab the duct tape from my dresser," I told him. "Top drawer."

He moved quickly and pulled out the tape, and all the while, Alex struggled, her protests coming out as muffled whines. As Jax pulled a strip from the roll, I picked her up and tossed her onto the bed. He and I worked together to get the tape over her mouth. I wound my belt around her wrists and anchored her hands to the headboard.

"Sit tight. We're not done yet." I got to my feet and threw on a pair of jeans and a T-shirt, and Jax led the way down the steps.

"A woman's here?"

"A hot blonde," he said. "I didn't let her in, and boy was she pissed."

Fuck.

Had to be Nikki. Once we touched ground, Jax folded the stepladder to the loft. I cast a glance toward the front door, dread twisting my gut for what waited on the other side.

"I tried telling her you were sleeping, but she wouldn't leave."

"I'm not surprised. If it's who I think it is, she doesn't have an agreeable bone in her body." I strode to the door, Jax on my heels, and pulled it open. She stood tapping a foot, arms crossed with a scowl on her face. "Who's the watchdog?" She jabbed a finger in Jax's direction.

"I think the real question," he said, lip curling, "is who the hell are you?"

"Who the hell am I?" She clenched her hands.

Double fuck.

"That's what I said, 'cause from where I'm standing, you're nothing but a stranger on my doorstep. A gorgeous stranger, but still."

She let out a growl of indignation, and I spoke before things escalated. "He's my roommate. What are you doing here, Nik?" And how could I get rid of her before the whole damn situation crumbled to the ground? I glanced over my shoulder and let out a small breath, as if I expected to find Alex standing behind me.

"I'm overwhelmed by the warm welcome." Nikki stepped forward, a sign she wanted to come inside. "I've been calling, or had you not noticed?"

"I noticed." Another glance behind me, another expelled breath. Thankfully, nothing but silence came from upstairs. "Can we meet somewhere in town later? Now isn't a good time."

She shook her head. "That's what I've been trying to tell you. You might want to avoid town for a while. Lyle's got it out for you, been saying all kinds of crazy things. People are starting to talk. He thinks you had something to do with that girl's death."

Jax stood straighter, his back rigid. I knew what he was thinking, but I wasn't about to let some small town gossip bring us down. I willed my face into a mask, though my pulse throbbed at my temples. "What girl?"

Her eyes widened. "You haven't heard?"

I arched a brow. "Heard what?"

"The girl who sent you to jail, her car was found in the river a few days ago. They said it was an accident, but Lyle thinks you had something to do with it." She raised her brows, and her forehead creased under honey blond wisps of bangs. "The timing's kind of convenient though. They found her car just twenty miles from here." She swept a hand between us. "And now you're here."

"You think I had something to do with it?" I dragged a hand through my unruly hair.

"No, I'm just saying I can see why some people might talk."

Jax folded his arms. "My head is spinnin' here, guys." He gave Nikki a slow once-over. "Who's Lyle, and who the hell are you?"

The first woman to catch his attention, and it would have to be the mother of my kid.

"Jax, this is Nikki."

"Well that tells me a lot."

I sighed. "We went to high school together. She's engaged to..." Fuck, he wasn't going to like this. "Lyle, the sheriff."

"*Perfect*." He gave me a pointed look, and I hoped Nikki didn't notice.

She took another step forward. "Can I come in, please? You took off so fast the other night—"

"Let's go for a walk," I interrupted as I wedged my

feet into my sneakers by the door. I glanced at Jax, and he gave an imperceptible nod. We were good at communicating without words. A dip of the head, a flick of the wrist, a furtive glance. We'd learned to talk in code long ago. He'd keep an eye on the prisoner while I chased off the threat.

I closed the door behind me and followed Nikki down the steps of the front porch. We walked in silence for a while, the hum of the highway and the roar of a freight train blending into one in the distance. "That yours?" I asked, gesturing toward the small fishing boat docked next to my larger form of transportation. It was a stupid question, but I didn't know what else to say.

"My dad's."

"How is he?"

"Not good. He's been drinking again, ever since Mom left."

Muttering the word "sorry" wouldn't cut it, so I said nothing. As we neared the dock, a few more feet down the sloped path, she slowed.

"I didn't come by because of Lyle."

"I figured as much."

"I mean, you always could handle yourself when it came to him."

I raised a brow, waiting for her to get to the point.

She twirled the engagement ring around her finger, a large princess cut diamond that looked as if it weighed down her hand. I wondered how a man on a sheriff's salary could afford such a ring. The whine of the train's engine grew louder, closer. She cleared her throat. "Thing is, Lyle doesn't know you're Will's father."

Her words stopped me cold. "Who does he think *is* his father then? Was there someone else?" The thought hurt more than it should.

She shook her head. "A few one-night stands when you were away at competitions or busy training, but no one around the time of conception. It was just you."

"But he doesn't know that?"

"Well, he didn't. I think he suspects now, since we met up for dinner. Small town and all that. You remember how it is. Nothing goes on in this place without everyone knowing about it."

I almost snorted. I guess living on an island gave me certain advantages, like being able to kidnap a woman and hold her prisoner. No one knew about that. Talk was one thing, but knowing was something else entirely.

"So what are you saying?" I threw my hands up in the air. "I don't know what you want from me. You didn't even tell me about him until a few days ago." I folded my arms to ward off the chill wafting from the river.

"Because you were locked up!" Wind whipped her blond hair into her face, and she angrily swiped it from her eyes. "The last time I saw you, I didn't recognize you, Rafe. I'd never seen you so pissed, so…so…"

"So what? Just say it." I stepped toward her, invading her space.

"So broken."

I took a deep breath. "Let's not do this shit. What do you want from me? You want me to step aside so you can have your perfect little family with Lyle?" I rolled my eyes. Lyle and picturesque family dynamics didn't mix. Who the fuck was Nikki kidding? I might have been dead to the world for the last eight years, or *broken*, like she said, but people didn't change. Not like that. If they did change, it was usually for the worse.

She lowered her head. "I don't know why I'm here, don't know what I'm doing anymore. Lyle is just getting nasty when it comes to your name. You need to watch your back, Rafe. He has a lot of power in this town. You already went down once for something you didn't do."

I stared at the river, recalling how Alex had fallen in the other night. I tried not to display any emotion. No clues, no ticks that would give away my guilty ass. "You should go," I said, knowing I was being rude but unable to stop myself. I had no explanation for Nikki. I didn't know what to do about my son. Fuck, I didn't know what *she* wanted me to do about him. "If you want Lyle to be his dad, I'll honor your wishes. Eight fucking years is a lot of time to miss. Maybe it's too late."

Why did that abrade so much? I'd barely glimpsed the kid, but the thought of letting him go, just as I'd found out about him, chiseled a hole in my heart.

She frowned. "You're his father. He should know you."

"He's probably in what…second grade now?"

She nodded.

"Kids talk, and they're mean as fuck. Maybe it's best if we keep it under wraps for now. Last thing I want is to disrupt his life by meeting him, then do it all over again by the talk that'll follow." I grimaced. The poor kid would take a lot of shit because of my time in prison.

"Okay." She turned and headed toward the dock, though I glimpsed the sadness in her eyes before she went. A few minutes later, after she'd started the motor and began across the river toward the boat ramp, I headed up the path to the cabin, my thoughts on Alex and whatever it was she was hiding. I didn't like it. Too much of the situation was on the verge of crumbling. I couldn't afford to be in the dark about anything, especially with a kid to think about.

Jax met me at the door, shrugging into his jacket as he stepped onto the porch. "Gotta go. I'll be back late tonight. Work is getting heavy."

"See you later." He and I needed to have a heavy talk, but first things first, Alex was going to spill, and seeing the river, remembering how absolute her fear was, would give me the perfect leverage to make her stubborn ass bend.

17. INTERROGATION

ALEX

The tape was hot and sticky over my mouth, and the feeling of being smothered almost put me into panic-mode. I kept my mind focused on whoever had landed on Rafe's doorstep, relieved that it wasn't Zach. A woman, Jax had said. Whoever she was, would she find me here? The idea of freedom unsettled me. I'd never stood on my own two feet. Someone had always told me what to do, who to see, who not to see, even what to eat. That was especially true once Dad found out about the anorexia. Rafe imprisoning me on this island had sent my life into a tailspin, but it was the most free I'd felt in a long time. If my captor had been anyone else, I'd feel differently.

The ladder dropped, and I tensed, wondering whose

head would pop through the opening. Rafe climbed into the loft and pulled up the stairs, effectively shutting the door to the outside world. It was just us. No rescue person in sight. He stomped toward me, and I tried not to flinch as he yanked the tape from my mouth. He released my hands and dragged me from the bed by my hair.

"What's going on?" I gasped, thrown off by his foul mood. Rafe wasn't the happiest guy on the block, but something had him worked up. "Who was here?"

"You've been lying through your deceitful little teeth, and it's gonna stop." He let go of me long enough to pull his shirt over his head and shed his jeans. I was still trying to process that he'd stripped naked when he shoved me in front of him and propelled me toward the bathroom. He picked up his belt on the way, and I dug in my heels, shaking as images of all the things he could do with that strap of leather popped into my head.

"What are you doing?" I didn't like where this was going, especially when he slammed the door behind us and bent me over the granite counter, wrenched my arms behind me, and wound that belt around my wrists. He moved away, and the sound of rushing water filled me with horror. I ran for the door.

He jerked me back, hand fisting my hair, and turned me toward the bathtub, my back to his front. His hand clamped down on my shoulder. The tub was huge, big enough for two and deep enough for an adult to drown in.

"What are you gonna do?" I twisted my neck to look at him, but what I found in his expression sent icy terror through my veins. A resolute line took hold of his mouth. My body quaked as the tub filled, and goose flesh erupted on my skin. He didn't answer my pleas and questions, and he didn't shut off the water until it reached the rim. The sudden onset of silence brought my fear to an all-time high. I tried to pull air into my lungs but failed.

He stepped around me, and my head jerked forward as he lifted a foot into the water. "Get in," he ordered once he stood fully in the tub.

"Don't do this!" I didn't recognize my voice—it echoed off the walls in thundering panic.

He yanked on my hair, and I slammed my knee on the porcelain with a yelp. "You did this," he said, "and you can come in willingly or I can drag you in, but one way or another, you're getting in this fucking tub."

Lifting a trembling leg, I stepped over and straddled the edge, and he pulled me in the rest of the way. He folded into a sitting position, back against the opposite end of the faucet, and brought me to my knees. I began to cry, big drops of salt that disappeared into the water enclosing me up to my belly button. It sloshed over the side with the smallest of movements. The whole time, his grasp on my hair never loosened.

"Scoot closer," he said, spreading his legs. I walked on

my knees and fit between his, and he pulled me lower, forcing me onto my haunches until the undersides of my breasts brushed the water's surface. My lips parted, breaths escaping in shaky bursts as our gazes tangled. He held me captive inside my worst nightmare, with the hold of his hand in my hair, the belt looped around my wrists behind me, and water rippling and stirring from the way my chest heaved.

I knew what he was about to do, and a sob bubbled up, tearing from my throat as I sensed the mere inches separating my mouth from the abyss. I didn't dare glance down, didn't dare break free of his stare. The nightmares I'd had as a kid came rushing back, more vivid than they had in years, and I hyperventilated, remembering the suffocating terror, the blackness and how I'd been helpless to save myself. That dream had tortured me, and the only way I'd woken up was by letting out a scream I never remembered, though my mom had described it as the most chilling thing she'd ever heard.

"Please don't. Oh God, please, Rafe!"

His expression was passive, tightly held in check, and that only added to the horror, until his smooth voice settled over me like a warm blanket. "Calm down. Deep breaths, Alex."

I inhaled, drawing air into lungs that didn't want to work right. He instructed me to do it again, and I repeated the exercise for several minutes, adding the calming ritual of counting until I no longer sounded like an asthmatic that had run a marathon.

"That's better. Hyperventilating isn't going to help you with this." He pulled my hair, bringing my face toward his submerged lap. "Don't even think of biting me."

"No! No!" I screamed. "Stop!" The last word cracked, as did the final thread of my composure. I thrashed, hair pulling painfully at my scalp as he pushed my head down.

"Take a deep breath. You're gonna need it."

I did at the last second before my face broke the surface and he pushed his erection into my mouth. I couldn't think beyond closing my lips to keep water from rushing down my throat.

He flexed his fingers in my hair and bobbed my head up and down in quick yet controlled movements that kept pace to the seconds ticking in my head. My heart beat much faster, at an insane speed that made my chest hurt, and I mentally chanted two words, over and over again.

Don't panic.

His salty flavor hit my taste buds, but before he came, he pulled me up. With a huge gasp, I sucked in air, hoarded it as if I'd never breathe again. Water trickled down my face in rivulets, lost to the locks of hair clinging to my nose and lips, and I fell into the sea of his eyes.

"Tell me what you're hiding." His tone left no room for maneuvering. I was in deep water, figuratively and literally, because he wasn't going to let this drop.

When I didn't answer, he yanked on my hair again, bringing me toward the water, and I cried, "Wait!"

"I'm done waiting, sweetheart."

With a violent downward thrust, he shoved me under the water once more, and I fastened my lips around his cock. He pushed against my tongue, and water forced its way down my throat. Lungs on fire, wrists burning at my back, I fought him, my whole body tense and vying for survival. Logically, I knew he wouldn't kill me, at least, I didn't think he would, but I was smack in the middle of fight or flight and trying to do both simultaneously.

Pockets of air escaped my nose and mouth, bubbling to the surface as my dark hair floated around me. My pleas came out as muffled rumbles. I was at the end of my ability to hold my breath and experienced the same panic I had when I'd fallen into the river. I was considering biting him, and weighing the consequences, when he yanked me up.

"Tell me why you accused me!"

"It was Zach!" I sobbed, gasping for air, coughing uncontrollably, and trying not to hyperventilate all over again as my brother's name rang in my ears.

Rafe froze, his eyes going wide. "You're lying."

If I had any reason to be terrified of him, this was it —that tone which told me he'd submerge me again.

"Zach was my best friend," he said. "He wouldn't do

that."

"But he did…" Another sob burst free, and I closed my eyes so he wouldn't see the truth in them. "I didn't stop him."

"Fucking look at me! Why, Alex? Why would he… why would you go along with it?" He stood, water sluicing down his body, and stepped onto the rug. He dug both hands into his hair and pulled. "Why would you guys do that to me?"

I was openly bawling, and all the emotion I'd battled with for years erupted. I was Mt. Saint Helens, shooting ash of despair on anything and anyone around me. "He…he…"

"He what?" Rafe shouted. "Spit it out!"

"He was jealous!"

"Jealous of what? That doesn't make any sense."

"Don't make me say it. Don't make me tell you this." My head drooped, chin to chest, and my shame poured from me in gut-wrenching sobs. I wished I could stop the dam from bursting, hide it all from him, but I'd never felt more exposed in my life. "He couldn't stand the way I felt about you."

"Look at me, Alex."

I peeked up, watching with dread as he studied me for the longest seconds of my life. His mouth fell open. "*He* raped you?"

Unable to face him, I lowered my head again because

that was only half of it, and I couldn't bring myself to tell him the whole truth. It had started out that way, but then, at some point, I'd stopped fighting and my body had given in to Zach. My own step-brother. The step part didn't make it any easier to swallow. It was sick and disgusting, and Rafe knowing twisted in my gut like a tornado.

He pulled me from the tepid water, gathered me in his arms, and strode into the bedroom where he deposited me on the bed, sop and wet. Warm hands settled on my face, fingers pushing tangled hair back, and when I risked looking at him, I fissured in two.

"I didn't want it," I sobbed. "I didn't, I swear. I'm so fucked up, Rafe." Humiliation, swift and debilitating, washed over me, and I gagged, close to vomiting. I struggled with the belt holding my hands at my back. "Let me free! Please, I need free!"

As he worked at releasing my hands, I nestled my cheek against his chest and took deep breaths to stem another episode of hyperventilation.

"How did it happen?" He spoke in a perilous tone, and when he inched back, I wanted to recoil at the unyielding set of his jaw. "How did I get brought into it?"

"I-I had an abortion." I wiped my eyes, palms digging in as that horrible day flooded back. "Someone from the clinic leaked it. Dad found out and kept the story from spreading, but he was so furious—" My voice broke, and

I stared at his bunched shoulders, my face flaming even hotter. "He flipped, demanded to know who I'd slept with. That's when Zach pointed the finger at you." I squeezed my eyes shut. "He said you raped me. Said he couldn't keep quiet about it anymore." Rafe's silence was too disturbing, and when I opened my eyes to face his reaction, utter betrayal blanketed his expression.

"You went along with the lie." No question, no inflection in his words. Just cold, hard truth.

"I'm *sorry*," I said, a sob constricting my throat. "I didn't know what else to do."

"How about tell the fucking truth?"

I jerked back as his rage thundered over me. "I c-couldn't."

"Couldn't, or wouldn't?" He leaned over the mattress, arms supporting his weight as he dripped water all over the bed and me.

"Couldn't." Our gazes collided. "He said he'd kill you if I didn't keep quiet."

Closing his eyes, he dropped his head and let out a breath. The admission seemed to burrow beneath his rage. His body pressed into mine, and we stayed that way for a few seconds until he suddenly bolted and let out a roar I was sure reached every crevice of the cabin. He whirled around and all but flew into the wall, his fist slamming into it, again and again, until his knuckles dripped with blood.

18. DESTROYED

RAFE

She cried for me to stop, but I continued to beat my fist against solid log as memories flickered behind my eyes in red-hazed horror. Instead of me taking the abuse, it was her. Zach holding her down, violating her, smothering her cries as he rammed into her.

The images shifted, and I was back in prison, full of rage yet unable to do anything about it as they took turns fucking me while the guards let it happen. All this time, I thought she'd callously tossed me aside, but I hadn't known why. Knowing didn't resolve anything, didn't bring me closure, and it sure as fuck didn't absolve us of our sins. Knowing only made me feel worse, because she'd suffered in silence out of fear for me.

I risked a glance at her, searching her expression for signs of duplicity. I'd rather find she was lying than accept what she'd told me as truth, but the same harrowing pain I'd seen in the mirror, day after day for the past eight years, haunted her face. I had trouble reconciling the Zach I remembered with the picture she painted. We'd been close, fiercely competitive but like brothers, and to find out such vile poison ran through his veins, that he'd hurt his own sister and threaten me…I couldn't comprehend it.

I dropped my bloodied fist, and it was a miracle my hand wasn't broken. Her whimpers tore through me as I staggered into the bathroom, heart pounding so fucking hard, I thought it would rip from my chest and tumble to the floor. Flinging the door to the medicine cabinet open, I pulled out gauze and wound it around my hand, but my head was still back in the bedroom with her, still wrapped up in the waves of shame that emanated from her being.

I couldn't get enough air into my lungs, especially when I laid eyes on the bathtub. Water still pooled around it, evidence of my torture methods. What I'd done to her in order to get the truth…now I wanted nothing more than to undo it, to go on believing she'd been a spoiled teenager, pride bruised over rejection. Just a selfish kid who'd flung out a single lie without giving thought to the destruction she'd cause.

Swallowing hard, I brought my injured hand to my

throat, as if that would alleviate the need for air. I had to get out of there for a while, had to get my head on straight before I tried to straighten out hers. I almost laughed. How did one straighten out so many years of pain and betrayal?

She was huddling under the bedding when I returned to the room. I pulled on a pair of jeans, and the weight of her stare pressed on me, burned to my bones.

"Where are you going?" she asked.

"Outside." I shrugged on a T-shirt, then escaped the room and the desolation seeping from her gaze. Her soft cries followed me down the ladder, but I was in no shape to comfort her, especially since I was no better than her brother, no better than the men who'd raped me in prison. If only I'd stopped long enough to think of all the angles, past my fury, maybe I would have considered she was a victim in this.

I'd kidnapped a girl who at age fifteen had been helpless in a situation forced upon her. I'd punished her without knowing the whole fucking picture. It wasn't even the sex that bothered me, as she'd wanted it. It was everything else—like being a cold and heartless ass who'd used her fear against her, debased her, and made her feel like she meant nothing to me.

I stormed outside but didn't go far, as if an invisible line anchored me to the house, to her. I clenched my jaw with the need to find Zach and dismember his dick from his body, but I couldn't leave her alone, and it dawned on me that I couldn't confront him either. He thought she was dead.

Fuck.

The whole world thought she was dead. I balled my fists. I'd taken her, and it was too late to go back. I didn't want to go back. I wanted her, all of her—her pain and sorrow, her joy and triumphs, her orgasms and her agony when I held them at bay. But letting her go would be the *right* thing to do.

I glanced toward the cabin and stilled. She stood in the doorway, eyes red-rimmed and haunted, her body wrapped in my sheet. She'd just admitted to being raped by her own brother, yet I wanted to tear that sheet from her and throw her to the ground. The memory of her mouth around my dick in the bathtub hit me, as did the fact I hadn't reached orgasm. I was royally fucked up.

I crossed the distance, climbed the steps to the porch, and shoved past her. Her footsteps pattered on my heels as I entered the living room. She walked timidly, as if scared to make a sound. Slumping to the couch, I held my head in my good hand while my injured one dangled between my knees. She sank to the floor and took my bad hand in hers. It didn't seem to matter what I'd done to her, or what I would do to her—I was starting to believe she was incapable of flushing me from her system.

She unwound the gauze and brushed her fingers over

my swollen knuckles. "Does it hurt?"

"It's not bad."

"I'm sorry."

I angled my head and looked at her. "You didn't force my fist into the wall."

"I'm not just talking about your hand. I'm talking about all of it."

"Why didn't you tell me?" I asked. She inched away, gaze downcast. I grabbed her hand and pulled her near again. "If I'd known what he did to you—"

"It's my fault you didn't."

"It doesn't matter, Alex. I took every fucking thing that happened to me in the last eight years and dumped it on you." Holes riddled my soul, each one representing something I'd never get back. My father's funeral, the first years of my son's life, having my career snatched from me—all because of Zach's jealousy. Even knowing she was a victim didn't quench my thirst for her pain, and that made me the vilest form of a bastard. "I got off on hurting you." I stared at her long and hard so she'd understand just how screwed up I was. "I still want to hurt you, so fucking much."

Her breath escaped in a shaky sigh. She wiped underneath her eyes, though she tried to hide it.

I hauled her onto my lap, unable to contain myself, and settled her knees on either side of me. The sheet draped open, and her hot pussy smothered my lap through my jeans. My cock sat between us, hard and painful, a reminder we had unfinished business.

"It's all my fault," she said, clutching my shirt.

"You were just a kid. You need to know it *wasn't* your fault." I swallowed hard as memories of my own assault broke free. I'd learned to contain them, to continue getting out of bed every morning and living life without freezing whenever something—a smell, a sound, or simple touch—triggered the flashbacks. "Zach knew better. Fuck, he was my age, and I sure as hell knew better." I ran a hand through her hair, fingers catching in the tangles, and pulled. She winced, but I didn't stop. "For fuck's sake, he was your brother."

"*Step*-brother."

"I don't give a fuck." How it was possible for us to carry on this conversation with her naked and in my lap, my erection growing by the second, was beyond me. "He had no right to touch you." Instantly, I dropped my hand from her hair as my own words came back to me like a boomerang. "I'm no better. I shouldn't have taken you." And I sure as fuck shouldn't entertain the thought of bending her over the couch and pushing into her.

"I'm glad you did."

Did she not realize what she was saying? I'd put her through hell, and my dick wasn't done with her yet, not even close. "I *wanted* to take you." My gaze veered to her neck when she swallowed hard. I settled a hand around her throat, surprised when she didn't fight me. The compulsion to squeeze the breath from her beckoned. "I have a demon inside me. That's what happens when a man has dark tendencies and no outlet for them. I used to fight them out of me in the cage."

"Rafe." My name fell from her lips with a breathy sigh. I pressed a thumb against her collarbone where her pulse fluttered as fast as a hummingbird's wings.

I didn't want to think it, let alone say it, but fuck, somewhere inside me a conscience still pulsed. I had to set her free. Except I had no end game. I'd fantasized about taking her for years, had planned out every last detail, but I hadn't foreseen the need to let her go. I didn't think she'd run to the cops, as her guilt came off her in palpable waves, but where would letting her off this island leave me, besides my life in utter disarray? I cursed my fucking conscience and its bad timing. "This has to end, Alex."

"What are you saying?"

"I'm saying I'm letting you go." The words hung between us, and now that they were out there, I wanted to snatch them back. There were so many reasons *not* to keep her here, namely that she wasn't as guilty as I initially thought in sending me to prison. She'd played a part, but how much choice had she really had? Fifteen was young, much too young to deal with rape, abortions, and blackmail.

"Why?" she whispered, as if the thought of getting her freedom back was unbearable.

I moved my hand to the back of her neck and drew her close, aching to take her mouth. "Because I still want to hurt you," I said, my attention drifting to her parted lips, "still want you in ways that isn't right. By the time I'm done with you, you'll beg to be mine, and that's a bad idea."

"I want to be yours," she said without hesitation, as if she wanted to be my everything, as if the idea of my being done with her tortured her. What we shared was pure obsession, nothing more and nothing less, and it was the sweetest madness in hell.

I shook my head, trying to convince myself as much as her. "I can't keep doing this to you. I battled with myself enough before I knew Zach's part in this, but now…"

She averted her gaze, but not before new tears formed. Watching her emotionally withdraw pissed me off.

"What is it? What are you thinking?"

"Nothing."

I clutched her jaw and forced her to look at me. "What are you holding back?"

"Nothing," she said again, though I saw the lie in her eyes.

"You need to be straight with me, on all of it, because

I'm so fucking close to hunting his ass down and killing him." The need to make him pay for what he'd done to her, for what he'd done to me, was strong and growing stronger with each second she tried to hide shit from me. And he would pay. Someway, somehow, I'd make him wish he'd never met me.

She shut her eyes to the tears slipping down her face, and I was a bastard because I wanted to taste them.

"Just tell me, sweetheart." Before I lost control and gave in to the boiling need inside me, to the demon that gnashed his teeth and almost broke free at the sight of her pain.

"He made me come."

"You got off when he raped you?" I wasn't surprised, not if the way she'd responded to me was any indication.

"Yes." She blinked several times but the flood had started and wouldn't stop. Her chest heaved with rising sobs. She didn't even try to pull away. She fucking sat in my lap, her chin trapped in my grip, and let me witness her shame. "He's been fucking me for years. I'm not as innocent as you think."

Her deviant nature pulled at me like a habit I couldn't quit. I took her mouth with greed, forcing her lips apart and thrusting my tongue inside. No build up, no closed-mouthed kisses to ease us into it. We plummeted into a full-on mouth fuck. With a deep moan, she pushed her tongue against mine, and I sucked her deeper, tasting her flavor and her tears.

Her needy fingers sifted through my hair and yanked, and I thought I'd die if I didn't taste more of her. Her perky tits with nipples partially obscured from the sheet, her belly button where I ached to dip my tongue. Her drenched pussy. I wanted to work her body until she begged, then push her further, making her scream and writhe with the need to come. I held her by the nape, placed my bloodied hand at the small of her back, and locked her in my kiss.

The issues between us didn't matter. Nothing mattered so long as she surrendered her soul to my demon and let him devour her. That single thought was powerful enough to make me pull away. I wouldn't let him finish her off. She'd been used and abused by her own brother, no one around to protect her. I'd be damned if I destroyed her too.

I pushed her from my lap. "This isn't happening." I rose to my feet, silently cursing as she folded the sheet around herself in shame, and adjusted my pants.

"W-what are you doing?" she asked as I headed toward the loft. Her bare feet scampered after me.

"Getting you some clothes." Until Jax and I figured out what to do with her, I wasn't going to tempt myself with her naked body. I climbed the steps and marched to my dresser, where I'd stashed a couple of outfits in her size. I pulled out a T-shirt and a pair of jeans and tossed them at her.

"Rafe…please." Her voice cracked on a sob. "Don't push me away. I need you."

"I'm the last person you need." I stumbled toward the bathroom without looking at her, my heart in my throat, and prepared myself for a long, cold shower and sex with my own fucking hand.

19. AGONY

ALEX

"What'd you do to him?" Jax asked. He sat across the table from me, working on his second beer, his plate from dinner empty in front of him. Rafe had inhaled his food before returning outside to work in the yard some more. He'd found "things" to do all day, the type of mundane tasks that kept him away from me.

"Nothing," I said, my shoulders slumping.

"So you siting here, fully clothed, I might add, while he's out there attacking the shrubbery is a normal everyday occurrence? I won't even go into how no one said a word over dinner. I know him, and I know when something's off."

My gaze fell to the sweatpants and T-shirt I'd slept in.

Rafe had taken the couch, leaving his bed to me. I glanced through the window. The late afternoon sun beat down on him, and his naked torso glistened in the heat. I wiped sweat from my brow. Today had been a hot one. I followed the lines of his tattoos with my gaze, and he caught me staring. His mere glance made my panties damp. I'd brought myself to orgasm last night, surrounded by his sheets and smell, but the release had been empty and anti-climatic, only serving to make me want him more. I'd ached to have him next to me, inside me, his body indiscernible from mine. I wanted him to make me come, craved it, because as long as he withheld that gift, he withheld his forgiveness.

Jax rose with a sigh. He exited through the back door, leaving it open, and hopped down the stairs of the patio to where Rafe was indeed abusing the shrubbery. He dropped the clippers as Jax approached, and though I couldn't hear what they said, it looked as if they were arguing. Jax gestured toward me, his lips tight, and Rafe shook his head. They exchanged words for a few minutes, then Jax stomped into the kitchen with Rafe on his heels.

"This is gonna blow up in our faces and you know it," Jax said. "She'll go straight to the cops, man. Never trust a woman, especially *that* one. I thought you'd figured that out by now, or did she castrate you?"

"You think I want him to go back to jail?" I interrupted, clenching my teeth and matching his glare.

"Why not? You sent him there once, didn't you? What's to stop you from doing it again?"

"Fuck," Rafe said. "I'm just trying to do the right thing. She doesn't belong here."

I sat up straight, my mouth dropping open, and I was about to protest when Jax spoke.

"What changed? Is she a rotten lay?"

Rafe's fist shot out and caught Jax in the nose. "Watch your fucking mouth."

"What the hell, man! We're really doing this over a chick?" Jax grabbed a paper towel from the counter and staunched the blood.

"We're doing this because you're not listening! Things have changed. She's gotta go."

"I'm not going anywhere," I said, and they both stopped and stared. I stood, gathered the dishes, and moved to the sink with as much calm as I could manage. "I've got nowhere to go, Rafe." What I didn't say was how I'd rather eat glass than leave him.

Jax sighed heavily, blowing his shaggy hair from his eyes. "I'm not sticking around to argue about it. If it's gonna blow, it's gonna blow. I'm not staying around for the explosion." He pointed a finger at Rafe. "Just think about it. If you let her go, we can kiss our freedom goodbye. I don't give a shit what she says otherwise." He tossed the soiled towel into the trash, spit out a mouthful of blood, and grabbed another paper towel on his way to the door. "Besides, you're never getting her outta your system. You took her, so deal with it. She's yours."

"Jax, wait—"

The door slammed on his exit, and the echo made the silence between Rafe and me that much louder. I was frozen, afraid to turn around and look at him. A chair scraped across the hardwood, and I heard him settle into it. Not knowing what else to do, I loaded the dishwasher as questions roared in my head, feuding with each other until one finally broke free.

"Did you tell him about Zach?"

"No, but I should have. He has a right to be pissed. His ass is on the line too. If I let you go—"

I spun around. "I don't want you to let me go!"

He jumped to his feet and knocked over the chair. "Have I not made you suffer enough? Fuck, Alex…" His voice cracked, with guilt and regret. I didn't deserve either.

With a growl, I hurtled a dish through the air and jumped when glass rained to the floor in a grating symphony of fury. "We already went over this. I got off on it! While you were in prison, being *raped*"—I choked on the word—"he was fucking me." I sank to the hardwood, knees to my chest, and hid my face behind my palms. "You should hate me. I hate me."

His footsteps thundered across the hardwood, and he yanked me up by the hair. "You don't *get* it," he snarled. "I want you off this damn island, far away from me, because I *don't* hate you." His fist clenched my strands, and he lifted until I stood on my toes. "Seeing your mouth twisted in pain, watching you battle the need to fight me, it *fucking turns me on*."

My lips parted, breaths coming in soft pants. I widened my stance, wincing again when the pull of his grip became unbearable. I slid a hand beneath the waistband of my sweats and dipped into slick heat. "All you have to do is glance at me, and it makes me wet." I lifted my fingers and pressed them to the hard line of his mouth, bathing his lips with the evidence of my arousal. "But when you're rough like this"—I gasped as he jerked my head back and sucked my fingers into his mouth—"I swear I'm gonna break if you don't fuck me."

His eyes met mine, holding me prisoner as his tongue darted between middle and forefinger. He bit down, watched my reaction, and when I didn't recoil, he let my fingers slip from his mouth.

"I'm giving you one chance to walk away." He let go of my hair and retreated. "You'll never hear from me again, never see me again."

I followed his backward motion. "How can you think I want that? I want you, Rafe." To make my point, I cupped his erection though his jeans.

He clamped his fingers around my wrist. "You're pushing it."

"What are you gonna do? Strip me naked? Lock me in the cellar again? Paddle me?"

"No," he said with a scowl, "but I can choke you, or better yet, I can drag your ass into the tub and make you suck me off."

I fought against his hold and stumbled, my heart pounding an erratic tune. "You wouldn't."

He tugged me close until our chests smashed together. "You know I would. No delusions, sweetheart. It's decision time. Stay or go?"

"Stay." The alternative of never seeing him again, of never experiencing his kiss or the possessive way his body claimed mine, that was something I wasn't willing to give up. If taking the pain he needed to inflict would grant me freedom from the burden of my guilt, would grant him relief from his own pain, then I'd take whatever he dished out.

He hefted me into his arms and strode to the stepladder. I slid to my feet, shuffling them with impatience as he brought the stairs down. As soon as we reached the loft, he pulled me against him, my back to his front.

"I'm gonna make you beg for it, gonna make you cry until you can't breathe for wanting me."

"Too late."

"Do you understand why you reached orgasm with him?"

I bit my lip, nodding, my mouth trembling as the memories surfaced. "Because I'm fucked up."

"So am I, and we're gonna be fucked up together, but I want you to answer something first."

I peeked at him over my shoulder. "What is it?"

"Did you crave him the way you crave me?" He grabbed my thigh and lifted, urging my foot around his calf. "Did your body ache and throb for him"—he slid a hand inside my sweats, fingers dipping into the inferno raging inside me—"the way it does for me?

"Never," I groaned, pushing into his palm.

"Then drop the guilt and shame. He exploited the way you're wired, used it against you. I'm gonna make you fucking embrace it."

He moved around and jerked my pants down my legs. My panties went next, ripped to shreds by his fingers. He fisted the collar of my tee in both hands and pulled until it split in two, right down to my navel. I stared at him in wonder, mouth hanging open.

"Rafe—"

"Don't talk. Just feel."

I felt, all right. He pushed the tattered shirt from my shoulders and slid my bra straps down my arms. He lowered the satin cups until my breasts tumbled out, and somehow, leaving the garment on made the act more forbidden. I felt the weight of his gaze on me, his tongue darting between lips I craved, and I would have given anything to have his tongue on my skin, but he didn't taste, didn't touch. He only looked, and looked some more until I thought I'd explode from his stare alone.

"Get on the bed."

I stumbled back, legs too shaky to do anything else, and fell onto the mattress. I reached behind me to unclasp the bra, but his growl stilled my hands.

"Don't do anything unless I tell you to, understand?"

I nodded.

"Stand on your knees, hands behind your back."

I obeyed without hesitation, barely containing the excitement bubbling in my stomach. He closed the distance slowly, a predator with prey in his sights, and peeled the clothing from his body as he went. Jeans, gone, on the floor. A step later, boxers flew into parts unknown. He climbed onto the bed behind me, and I gasped when he splayed a tattooed hand on my abdomen, fingers reaching past my navel toward the crevice of pulsing arousal. He yanked my head back, until my eyes aligned with his chin, and lowered his head. His lips opened over my collarbone, feverish and hungry, teeth scraping tender skin. My nipples hardened into two tight buds, and my skin broke out in goose bumps from head to toe. I'd never been so worked up, so ready to fly apart from touch alone.

He teased upward, across my cheek to the edge of my mouth, his stubble leaving a rough path in his wake. His fingers slid inside me. I moaned, a second away from begging for his kiss.

"You're so wet. Drenched and hot." He let go of my hair and gripped my throat, holding me prisoner against his body. His gaze fell on my mouth, and he couldn't hide it—the need to kiss me.

This man brought out so many emotions, but above all else, intense yearning. I'd rip myself apart to get to him. "I need you, Rafe," I whispered, eyes threatening to spill so much more than tears. He saw everything, laid bare before him just as my body was. I gave him my submission, opening my thighs wider to his touch, arching into his possession of my throat, my breasts jutting forward, unabashedly on display. "I need you so much."

"Tell me something," he said, his fingers sliding in and out of my pussy in slow ecstasy.

"Anything."

"Have you been with anyone else?"

"Just you." I wouldn't mention Zach. He didn't count, and from the hard glint in Rafe's eyes, I'd said the right thing.

"Good." He groaned, then his mouth was on mine, parting my lips with desperate urgency, tongue thrusting inside as his fingers fucked me. His mouth tasted of the strawberries he'd eaten earlier.

I couldn't be contained. I had to touch him, or I'd

combust. I shoved my fingers into his hair and clutched him as if I'd never let go, urging his tongue deeper into my mouth. Kissing him from this upside down angle unraveled me, destroyed me, and I never wanted to be whole again. Not if coming unglued in his arms meant feeling this way for even a second longer. I was his, every frayed thread of my aching soul.

"Fuck, Alex," he said, wrenching his mouth from mine. His erection jabbed my ass.

"I need you. Please."

"I'll fuck you when I'm ready. Put your hands behind your back."

"Ahhh!" I screamed, fists tightening in his hair.

He flipped me to my back and forced my hands to the mattress. His body towered above, trapped me with his dangerous masculinity, and I was a willing prisoner. I freely turned over the key to the metaphorical chains that bound me to him.

Rafe's dark head dipped to my breasts, and he tugged the bra cups down with his teeth. I cried out, unprepared for the hard bite on my nipple. Sharp pain radiated through me, gathering strength until it coiled low in my belly. I arched my spine, muscles taut when he moved to my other breast and clamped his teeth into tender flesh.

I hissed in a breath to keep from howling, writhed beneath the punishing attention of his mouth, but he didn't stop. He wouldn't stop. Mercy was his to give, his to withhold. I'd given up my one and only chance at freedom.

His fingers became painful vises around my wrists, holding me down and rendering my struggle useless. He wedged my legs apart and settled his cock at my entrance, pushed in the tiniest bit, then withdrew.

"Please…" I was going to die. If it was possible to drop dead from being teased and tortured so excruciatingly, to be in a constant state of arousal, only heightened by the pain he kept unleashing on my body, then I was a goner. "Rafe, for God's sake, fuck me."

"You're gonna give me everything." He raised his head and looked at me. "I'm gonna choke you. Still wanna stay?"

I bit my lip to keep it from quivering. "Do I have a choice?" I only asked to test him, to see how far I could push. If he was still willing to let me go, then I'd know some part of him still battled with his former self. That guy would always give a choice, always do the right thing, even when he was being fucked in the process.

He let go of my wrists and wrapped his hands around my neck. "Your chance for freedom has passed. Hold onto the bars. If you let go, I won't let you come."

I grasped cold, hard metal and held on tight. "Why do you need this?" I asked, the question guttural because my airway felt so narrow under the weight of his hands.

"Choking your beautiful neck gets me harder than

fuck." He leaned down with a barely contained groan, and our faces lingered inches from each other. "Nothing else gets me off so good." He paused for a beat, tilting his head. "But it's about trust too, about you knowing your place. Your pleasure comes with a price. I want every piece of you, every time."

He pushed his cock in slowly and trembled. "I mean it. Let go of those bars, and I'll make you suffer for a week."

I gripped them with all I had, determined to obey him, to prove I could be what he wanted, what he needed, but my heart drummed too loudly. If not for the sensual rhythm he set, shallow thrusts that teased, barely pushing into the wetness dripping onto the sheets, I would have panicked as the pressure on my throat increased.

His sensuality came as a surprise, and I surrendered to it. Through the haze, I saw his face tighten in a mixture of pain and pleasure, and I realized being face-to-face like this, with our bodies coming together in tender agony—something about it hurt him on a deep level. I saw it in the way his hooded eyes drew me in and demanded I bear some of the anguish. Mine drifted shut, because watching him watch me, specks of the past shining in his gaze, tore me to shreds.

"Don't hide from me. I want your eyes."

"It hurts to see you like this." It was easier to face what I'd done when he was angry, righteous, contemptuous. Not while he bared the part of himself he kept hidden. My heart grieved because he was loving my body while showing how I'd destroyed every facet of his being.

"Open your fucking eyes."

I lifted my lids and the connection between us was unbreakable. Neither of us looked away as he pushed to the hilt. He slid in and out, his movements still tender, yet his hands were unrelenting. They tightened further, constricting my airway as an orgasm built, as his neared the brimming point.

"Let me come," I begged.

"Not until you're screaming for it." He drove his cock in with renewed fervor, and we both cried out. "Not until you can't breathe," he said with a groan. "Fuck, I want you waking up on fire." His hands squeezed, and I resisted fighting him, holding so tightly to the bars, my knuckles cramped.

Our gazes remained locked together as he choked the air from me. The moment was surreal, his eyes sparkling like emeralds for those few seconds when I turned my life over to him. Everything around him narrowed to black, and there was only him in my vision, in my world, in my heart. I opened my mouth, needing to say his name, but it wouldn't come out.

"Don't fight it. Just a couple more seconds—"

When I came to, his name a sigh on my lips, I felt his

head disappear between my legs. He flattened his tongue on my clit and pressed hard. I squirmed and bucked, limbs quaking high on his shoulders, and gasped for breath. I wanted to claw at my neck, but my fingers remained one with the headboard. I wouldn't let go, no matter what.

"Rafe!" I rasped. "I need to come. Let me come." I repeated the plea until it became a continuous prayer. I didn't know how he did it, but he was skilled at keeping me on edge. His tongue and fingers brought me higher, and my cries tore through the loft. Nothing on Earth felt as good as him between my thighs, licking and sucking, entering a finger and curling it just the right way.

Holy fuck.

He entered another finger, moved his mouth to my inner thigh, and bit down. His fingers worked me as I arched above the bed with a shriek. His teeth sank in deeper and that bite spread through me until I was out of control and lost in helplessness. He brought a hand up and twisted my nipple, eliciting a full-on scream.

Don't let go of the bars…whatever you do, don't let go.

"Please…please…give it to me."

He pulled away and sat on his haunches, and I cussed at him, out of my mind as blood pumped to my core and begged for release. My foul-mouthed rant seemed to amuse him. "You're an instrument I like to play. I can strum you for hours. I like you this way—wild, desperate, and fucking insane with lust."

"Will you ever forgive me?" I squirmed as salty frustration drenched my cheeks. "I'll do anything. Please, I need you."

"Forgiving you won't erase the last eight years. I can't just wipe that shit from my head."

I flushed with shame, acutely aware of how I was spread before him, wet between my thighs while his mind dwelled in past horrors. "I'd do anything to go back, Rafe."

His brows furrowed over contemplative eyes. "What am I to you? Some fantasy you held on to all these years? What do I mean to you?"

I groaned. "You're my beginning, my end. You're my everything."

Slowly, his face relaxing in something close to tenderness, he slid up my body and folded me in his arms. "You sure know how to twist the knife, sweetheart." With a heavy sigh, he pushed into me again. His strokes were just right. His hand on my nape, holding me in place as he nibbled at my neck, was just right. His body enveloped mine, like a cherished present he was carefully unwrapping.

He gripped my neck, sank his teeth in, and I screamed when the tsunami began. I pulsed and clenched around him, ached long and deep, and I couldn't stem the howl erupting from my being. I clutched his hair, no longer able to hold on to metal when I could hold on to him, not with the way I was coming. And just as the tide ebbed, another wave crested. He never stopped thrusting, didn't slow or quicken his pace. He worked my body as if I were made for him.

"Do it again," he said with a gruff quality that was sexy as hell. "Howl for me. Come undone. I'll put you back together."

I screamed again, my face a mess of sweat and tears, and grasped his shoulders, my fingernails biting into hot, damp skin. "I fucking love you," I choked as the last ounce of strength fled. I was gelatinous skin and bones in his embrace.

"No, stay with me." He still moved inside me, and his lips mashed against his teeth as he neared orgasm. He dropped his head into the crook of my shoulder, smothered a deep groan, and emptied into me.

Time stilled, seconds ticking in an endless loop while we held each other, and eventually our breathing slowed. Twined together in sweat, twisted in each other and in the sheets, the charged air blanketed us. I didn't know how much time had passed, but his face took up space only inches from mine. I breathed in when he exhaled, our chests dancing together to the same beat. My skin tingled and sparked from head to toe, and I shivered because he was still nestled inside me, his erection growing by the second.

"I'm still fucking hard. I can't get enough of you." He pressed me into the mattress and pinned my arms above my head. His need to control no longer scared me. If anything, it made me feel more connected to him, more alive. By giving him this, I felt I was giving him back a small piece of himself. I'd never be able to atone for my sins, for the years of torment I'd put him through, but I could do this, could give him every broken piece of me.

"I've never felt this way before," I whispered.

"What way?"

"Like you. Like I can't get enough."

"My insatiable little slut." His lips curved against mine, taking the sting out of the insult. Unlike when Zach said it, the word held different connotations when coming from Rafe's lips. Pride, possessiveness. His fingers tightened around my wrists. "My sexy little slut. I've waited so fucking long to be inside you." His free hand circled my jaw, and his lips and tongue battled with mine endlessly. We came up for air, and he bit into my shoulder.

I drew in a breath between clenched teeth.

"Does my need to hurt you scare you?" he asked.

"No."

"This is nothing, Alex. I have some really fucked up fantasies, things I've never tried with anyone."

I should have felt at least marginally afraid by his admission, but I could only grasp a single detail—he'd never done the things he wanted to do with me.

"Like what?"

"That's a conversation for another day."

"Rafe," I groaned.

"I'll need to make you cry. Often. I love the taste of your tears."

"My heart's already bleeding them. Do what you need. I'm yours."

"You're gonna regret being mine."

A tremor of fear speared through me. The way he said it, with unmitigated certainty, took my breath. He didn't need to use his hands to steal my lifeblood.

He pulled out of me and crawled to his hands and knees. "Turn over."

I flopped to my stomach and shivered as chills traveled over my back.

"I'm not done with you, not even close."

20. INTRUDER

ALEX

Something was wrong. It pulled at the edges of my mind and demanded I take notice. I reached for Rafe, but my fingers grasped empty space. His side was bereft, though the sheet still radiated his body heat, so he couldn't have been gone long. I jolted upright, eyes blurry, and blinked. We must have fallen asleep after our second round of sex.

The loft was the way we'd left it, though it was cast in shadow, indicating the sun had set. Once my eyes adjusted, I noticed the ladder was closed and the bathroom door shut. Darkness seeped from underneath, so he wasn't using the toilet. Grabbing the sheet and surrounding my body with it, I tiptoed to the ladder and let it drop to the floor with a loud clank that made me jump. I was about to call out his name when another voice stopped me.

"Who's here?" Zach's question thundered up the stairs, and I slapped a hand over my mouth to keep from crying out.

"Just some girl I hooked up with. Listen, we should talk about this when you're sober." Rafe's calm tone poured over me like warm honey, and I let out a breath until it sank in that Zach was really here, just a few feet away. And he was drunk.

I stumbled back, gouging my fingernails in my arm, and lost precious seconds as I thought of my brother discovering my presence. They exchanged more words but none of them penetrated. I was too frozen in a waking nightmare of Zach finding me in nothing but a sheet. He'd go irate and kill Rafe. Frantic, I searched for my clothes and found my sweats on the floor. The T-shirt was ruined, so I jerked a drawer open and grabbed a shirt that was sure to swallow my tiny frame. I stepped lightly across the room, gritting my teeth when the floorboards creaked, and listened, remaining out of sight.

"You're a fuckin' liar! I know she was on her way here."

"What are you talking about?" Rafe's voice held steady, but even so, I balled my hands. He could handle himself, I knew he could, but I couldn't get the memories out of my head. Zach was insane when jealous and irrational, and it was like watching a lion let loose all its ferocity onto a weaker species.

Rafe had taken him down so many times during their matches, but this was real. This wasn't a training session or a controlled fight inside a cage with screaming fans crowding around to watch. This was bad.

"The little bitch was running straight to you. I'm not stupid. Did she call you? Tell me what she said, every word. I need to know."

"Seriously, Zach. I never heard from her."

"She's always wanted you, and now she's"—his voice broke—"gone. Just like that. This is *your* fault! I swear to God, I'll tear you to pieces if you don't tell me what she told you."

"I was convicted of raping her, remember?" Rafe's tone barely concealed a lethal edge. "So why would she come here? That doesn't make any sense."

God, he was clever, and it made me love him all the more. Zach couldn't argue with him, not without incriminating himself.

"Then why'd they pull her car from the river down the fucking highway?" he yelled.

"I don't know."

"I can't go on without her," Zach choked. "I won't."

"C'mon, man…" Rafe's voice faltered, and my spine stiffened. Something had him scared. "Put the gun down."

I gasped, then slapped my hands over my mouth, but it was too late. The sound echoed in my ears like a blaring siren, and I was certain Zach heard it.

"Tell your *hookup* to get her ass down here."

"This is between you and me," Rafe said. "I barely know her. She doesn't need to be part of this."

"Get down here now!" Zach shouted.

I stumbled down the stairs, my legs shaking so badly, Rafe steadied me to keep me from sprawling on my ass. He pushed me behind him, but not before I saw Zach's eyes bulge.

"The hell?" He jabbed the gun in Rafe's direction. "Lex?"

"Go home," I told him, hating how my voice quaked. "I called the cops. Th-they'll be here any minute." It was a lie, Rafe knew it, as I didn't have access to a phone, and I was positive Zach knew it too from the way I tripped over the words.

"Un-fucking-believable." Zach's bitter laugh made me cringe. "Do you think I give a shit about the cops? Let them come."

Rafe was strung so tightly, I worried he'd strike at any second, but he reached a hand behind his back and clutched mine, as if I could anchor him. "What do you want, Zach?" he asked.

"I want you dead."

I swallowed a sob and clung to Rafe's hand. "Please,

leave us alone."

Zach gestured at me with the gun. "Get over here."

"N-no."

Rafe's shoulders bunched, and his fingers squeezed mine.

"Now!" Zach staggered forward. "Get over here, or I swear to God, I'll shoot him."

A sob escaped, as I recognized the truth in his words. Even though he was wasted, a gun evened the playing field. He was much too close, and it wouldn't take a straight shot to hurt or even kill. I went to move away from Rafe, but he wouldn't let go.

"You're not touching her. You want to shoot me, do it, but you're not laying a hand on her."

"Don't test me!" Zach roared, raising the gun a few inches.

I yanked free and flung myself at Zach, clutching his shoulders, and the barrel pressed into my chest. "I'm here. Don't hurt him."

"What are you doing?" Rafe shouted.

"Stay back," Zach warned him. "Don't make me hurt her."

I couldn't see Rafe's reaction to my brother's threat, but Zach's lips thinned into a dangerous line. "Did you fuck him?"

"Zach," I pleaded, avoiding his furious gaze.

He gave me a rough shake with his free hand.

"Answer the question!"

"Yes!"

He spit at me, and I resisted the urge to inch back as I wiped my cheek on my sleeve. He'd only pounce on it, see it as a display of weakness. As long as I stayed between the gun and Rafe, Zach couldn't shoot him. Somehow, I had to get the weapon away from him.

"Why, Lex? Why can't you love me like I love you?"

"If you love me, you'll calm down and think about what you're doing." My words seemed to have the desired effect. He let out a breath, and I felt the gun slide down my chest by a few degrees.

"Of course I love you, baby. I'm the only one who loves you. He's just a fucking waste of space." He tried to push me to the side, but I clung to his jacket.

"Let's go," I said. "Right now. We'll get far away from here, just you and me." I inched a hand down his chest, disguising my aim for the gun as a caress.

Rafe jerked me back before I got close to the weapon and shielded me with his body. "Fuck no. You're not stepping foot out of here with him." Holding my hand tight with one hand, he gestured toward the gun with the other. "Why don't you put that down and fight me, like we used to, or are you too washed up to take me?"

With a snarl, Zach switched on the safety and jammed the gun into his waistband. "Bring it, asshole. I can take you in my sleep."

With the gun no longer a threat, and Zach too wasted to be a real challenge, Rafe wouldn't have a problem taking him down.

"You haven't been locked up with hardened criminals," Rafe said as he moved toward my brother, his grip slipping from mine. "I'm gonna rip you a new one for what you did to me, for how you raped your own sister, you sick fuck." He rolled his shoulders, his stance wide and hands balled at his sides.

I jumped back and slapped a palm over my mouth as he charged Zach. He grabbed him and brought his knee up, one, two, three times until Zach fell to his knees. Something insidious unleashed in Rafe, and it scared the shit out of me. I'd never seen him so unhinged. He pounded on Zach with his injured hand, but it didn't slow him down.

Zach countered the next onslaught of punches and managed to get an arm around Rafe's neck. I screamed, my heart in my throat as I watched them fight for survival. This wasn't a battle for something as inconsequential as a title. This was a battle for life. Rafe's, mine, even Zach's.

Rafe tried to turn into the choke hold, but my brother was high on adrenaline and obsession and wasn't about to let go. Rafe's face blanched, eyes rolling back, and I recognized the burn for air by the grimace on his face, certain it was the same expression that crossed mine whenever he choked me. Except Zach wouldn't stop at unconsciousness. He'd kill him, and not even a bloodstream full of alcohol would hinder him.

"Stop!" I pounced on his back and reached into his waistband, desperate to get my hands on the gun. I curled my fingers around the handle and jumped back, flipped off the safety, and held it in shaking hands, aiming at Zach's head. "Let him go!" I hoped he'd hear the steel in my voice, realize how serious I was, because if I had to choose between Rafe and him, it would be Rafe. "Now!" I shouted, steadying the gun, my finger on the trigger. "You know Dad taught me to shoot. I won't miss."

Zach scowled but let Rafe's limp body drop to the floor. "You're not gonna shoot me."

I fired a shot over his shoulder, thankful for all the times our father had taken me to the range. Zach put his hands up and backed toward the door. Rafe gasped for breath as he pushed to his hands and knees. My attention wavered from Zach for an instant, just long enough for him to flee through the front door.

Rafe rose to his feet, his breaths coming fast and hard. "Give me the gun."

The aftereffects of jumping my brother hit me, and the gun wobbled in my hand. "I-I…"

"C'mon, hand it over. He's gone now."

For how long?

Rafe took the gun and curled a hand around my

bicep. "I'm getting you out of here."

"W-where are we going?" Of course, I knew, but even with my brother on the run and posing a real threat, I couldn't stem the panic at the thought of leaving. "I can't do this."

"No choice. I'm getting you off this island."

I pulled against his hold, my heart pounding so hard, I thought my chest would rip open. "No! Please. Let's just call the cops." Even as the words left my mouth, I realized why he couldn't. The cops would come, and the island and cabin would become a crime scene. They'd find the prison down in the cellar and they'd start asking questions, namely why someone who was supposed to be dead was still very much alive. I struggled as he forced me from the house, down the porch, a few steps closer to the water.

"I need you safe," he said, "because I'm gonna fucking kill him."

I dug in my heels, bare feet sliding over dirt and rock. "You *can't*! You're not a murderer, Rafe!" He was too prone to guilt. I'd seen it firsthand. "It'll destroy you."

He picked me up and flung me over his shoulder, and I kicked, clawed, screamed, hit…all of it seemed to bounce off him as he strode toward the water.

"I'm doing this for you."

I screamed, coming unglued as he tossed me into a boat. The water terrified me, but as he unwound the rope anchoring me to the dock, that almost split me in two. "Come with me! Please, Rafe! Please—" I broke into unintelligible sobs, left with nothing to do but drift away from the island. From him.

"Alex!" he called as he let loose another boat—Zach's I guessed. It floated in the direction mine had. "You'll hit land a little ways upstream. Stay calm. I'll find you."

I nodded and squeezed my eyes shut. I couldn't speak.

"He won't hurt you anymore. Not when I'm through with—" A loud grunt tore through the night, and my lids popped open.

I scrambled to my knees as he battled with Zach for the gun. Holding both hands over my racing heart, I screamed Rafe's name. And I screamed and screamed some more when they fell to the ground and Zach beat him over the head with a rock. Rafe stopped struggling.

He wasn't fucking moving. The scene before my eyes crawled in slow motion as Zach pushed to his knees, then to his feet. He stepped back, body swaying, and aimed the barrel at Rafe's unmoving form.

OhmyGodohmyGodohmyGod…

I screamed at him to stop, but my voice cut out when the blast echoed off the mountains. I almost fell into the water, reaching, pleading, praying for Rafe to get up, but Zach kicked his body into the river.

My mouth opened, yet no sound came out. This wasn't happening. That shot was a car backfiring from the highway, or someone testing their illegal mortars a few weeks early of the Fourth of July. Any second now, Rafe's strong arms would pull him to safety and he'd beat the shit out of Zach.

But he didn't surface.

Zach dove into the water with a splash, and his strokes brought him straight for me with the stealth and speed of a shark. I could do nothing to save myself. Water lapped against the boat, paralyzing me. My fear trapped me, held me prisoner in my own mind, and Rafe...

He wasn't coming up, wasn't gasping for breath and diving after Zach.

My heart fractured, split wide open, and I didn't recognize the howl of agony spilling from my being. Zach pulled himself into the boat, his sodden clothing weighing him down, and shoved a hand over my mouth. I flailed as he wound an arm around my neck. I fought him with everything I had, even as my gaze fastened to the spot where Rafe had gone under. I longed to slip into the void after him, to vanish as he had. I didn't want to live if he didn't.

The headlights crawling along the highway, like pairs of lightening bugs, blinked out in my periphery, and the night narrowed to nothing, yet that empty spot in the river burned in my mind.

21. VANISH

RAFE

I jerked awake in the depths of icy water, kicked weak and useless limbs, and eventually broke the surface. Gasping, I pulled myself onto land with jittery arms and spewed water from my lungs, coughing until I puked. I rolled to my back, and the throb in my head made itself known. So did the fire in my left shoulder. The sky spun like a damn acid trip. Wet and itchy grass cradled my body, and I groaned as I ran my fingers along a nasty gash in my skull. I pulled my hand away and winced at the blood covering it. Too much blood.

Shaking uncontrollably, my heart rate doubled as I tried to sit up, but I couldn't get myself off the ground. The stars seemed to distance themselves, as if they knew

I'd suck the light out of them. I thought I heard someone scream, and something about that hysterical plea fisted my insides. What the fuck had happened to me? I recognized my dad's island, but why I was sprawled on it, hurt and bleeding, I didn't know. Another scream cut through the air, abruptly cut short as it carried in the night. Someone was in trouble, needed my help, yet I couldn't move…couldn't stay…awake.

Someone lifted me, followed by the unmistakable sway of a boat ride. A voice kept talking to me, telling me to hold on.

Almost there, buddy.

Almost where?

A horn blared, tires screeched, and frantic voices exchanged meaningless words because everything was meaningless. None of it made sense. Where was I?

Didn't someone need help?

A sharp pain stabbed my chest at the thought. I was unworthy, a sadistic ass who'd done horrible things…who had I done this to? And why would I do something so… what had I done? Why was trying to remember making my head throb like a fucking drum, pounded on by brutal drumsticks that inflicted the most horrid pain? I felt those strikes clear though my eyeballs to my teeth.

Hands grabbed my body and lifted, sliding me onto something cold and hard and bumpy. An engine rumbled to life. I groaned as I rolled, though an arm steadied me, as did the leg stretched out at my side.

A bright light woke me, searing my eyes and intensifying the throb at my temples, which kept time to the rhythmic beep that irritated my ears. I rubbed the blurriness from my vision and took in the small room. What the hell? Had I lost a fight, beaten so badly I'd needed hospitalization?

Why couldn't I remember?

Someone shifted on my left, and I found a guy slumped in a chair, his dark blond hair a mess on his head. His drawn face displayed signs of fatigue.

"Thought I'd lost you, man."

I blinked. Something wasn't right. He must have been in the wrong room, or confused.

I closed my eyes, but when I opened them, he was still staring at me, waiting for an answer. "Why are you here?"

"Seriously? We get into one fight and this is how you're gonna play it?" He brushed the hair from his brown eyes. "That's cold. If I hadn't come back, you would've bled to death. Lucky for you, you sonofabitch, it was a clean shot, so no permanent damage."

I blinked again, feeling as if I were missing several cards from the deck. "I don't remember. How long have I been here?"

Some of the anger left his shoulders. "You've been laid up three days. It was touch and go for a while. You lost a lot of blood, and they didn't know how long you'd gone without oxygen."

What the hell? No one choked me out. It just wasn't done. *I* choked my opponents.

"Must have been some fight."

He raised a brow. "That's a mild way of putting it. No one can piece together what happened." He gave me a heavy look, then lowered his voice. "Which is a good thing since *you-know-who* vanished, though I'd like to get my hands on whoever did this."

"What are you talking about?"

"Well, I'm guessing you let her go? There's been no sign of her since. I said I found you on the side of the highway, so the island is secure. No cops crawling it." He sighed. "So what *do* you remember? Because fuck, Rafe, I don't have a clue what happened out there."

I studied this tattooed stranger through squinted eyes, still having no idea who he was or what he was talking about, yet he acted as if he knew me. "Um, I remember seeing Nikki the other night." Hell, that girl could fuck a guy raw. My dick twitched as I remembered how she'd ridden me.

"How bad did you bump your head? Nikki showed up a few mornings ago. Close call too." He ran a hand through his hair. "I knew the risks when I signed on for this, but I gotta say it—these past few days have been a bitch."

"What?" Was he purposefully speaking in riddles? I'd fucked Nikki the night Zach and I had gone head-to-head. I was still on a high from winning that title, knowing my dream of fighting in the UFC was a real possibility now. As for the rest of what this guy at my bedside said, it made about as much sense as his presence.

I glanced around the room and tried to figure out what I was missing. Plain white walls, standard hospital machinery, and that fucking beeping that increased the throbbing in my head. Most notably, someone was absent. "Where's my dad?" I wasn't surprised my brother hadn't shown up. He was always too busy to differentiate his asshole from his mouth, and he'd never approved of my career anyway, but Dad would be the first one here.

The guy narrowed his eyes. "Something's not right…" He jumped to his feet and hit the call button.

"What are you doing?"

"Getting help, 'cause you're not acting like yourself."

"Dude," I said, "How would you know? I don't even know who the hell you are. No offense."

He collapsed back into the chair, eyes wide, and his panic penetrated my tough veneer. His reaction scared me, and I didn't know why.

"That is *not* funny," he said. "Cut the crap."

I shook my head. "Seriously, who are you?"

He pushed his hands through his hair. Three times now, he'd done that. Must be a nervous tick. "This isn't happening." His gaze bored into me. "Who's the President?"

"Of the UFC?"

"No! Of the fucking United States."

I furrowed my brows. "Bush, why?"

"Shit," he said, then dropped his head into his hands. A few seconds later, he looked up, his face taut with stress. "What year is it?"

"2006. What the hell is going on?"

"You've lost eight years of your life, man. That's what's going on."

Thank you for reading *Torrent*! If you enjoyed the story, please consider leaving a review, even a short note expressing your thoughts. Reviews mean the world to authors! *Rampant*, book two in the *Condemned* series, will be available in late October 2014!

BLURB FOR RAMPANT

Life is twisted. Cruel. After being ripped from the safe haven of Rafe's arms, my new kidnapper is waging a sick game. Unable to make my body do his bidding, he's resorting to psychological warfare. He'll bend my mind until I break, and when I do, that just might be my saving grace.

I'll forge through hell to get back to Rafe, body and spirit broken and bleeding, but I'm unprepared for what I find. He's done what I can't: he's erased eight years of pain and betrayal. I don't know how to bring him back to me, because bringing him back means ripping him to shreds all over again.

ACKNOWLEDGEMENTS

You'd think after finishing a book, writing the acknowledgements would be easy, but I think this is the hard part. I owe so many people heaps of gratitude in the creation of this novel. Firstly, I want to thank the readers. Consider my mind truly blown over your enthusiasm of my work. Without you guys, I would just be a writer stringing together words that impacted no one. I love reading your emails and messages on Facebook, and I guess I have a sadistic streak because when you tell me you've lost sleep from reading something I wrote, I have to admit to being thrilled. I've been there many times myself. Drink a cup of coffee, or five, and think of me. Cheers to my fellow night owls! :)

And that brings me to betas and bloggers. Let's call them the Amazing B's. Huge thanks to the following bloggers for your support: Amber and the girls at The Reading Room Blog; Becs and her crew at Sinfully Sexy Book Reviews; Kathy at Romantic Reading Escapes; and Cariad at Sizzling Pages Romance Reviews. I also want to shout out to the following promoting badasses: Debra at Book Enthusiast Promotions, Franny and Silvia at Dark World Books, Giselle at Xpresso Book Tours, and Natalie at Love Between the Sheets Promotions. There are countless other bloggers who deserve a thank-you—each and every one of you who work tirelessly to promote authors simply because you love books. I'm in awe of the work you put into your blogs and reviews. THANK YOU!

A million and one thank-yous to Pam Godwin and Amber for giving me invaluable feedback that helped turned this monster into something that didn't totally suck. I adore Pam and her style of critiquing. Her comments made me laugh-out-loud, and I'm honored that such a great wordsmith worked with me on Torrent. And Amber, who ripped my story to shreds in the best way possible and demanded a Rafe who wasn't such a pussy—you so rock! Knowing what you've been through lately and seeing the way you've picked yourself up to face each day, it inspires me. You've got strength, girl.

A heartfelt thank-you to Ann Everett, whom I "met" online three years ago (can't believe it's been that long). We've traded everything from publishing advice to critiques. You've got a gentle spirit yet such a naughty mind, lol! I love your work, and I'm so thankful for all the little things you caught in this manuscript that no one else did.

I also want to thank Crystal, my own real-life cheerleader, for putting up with long car rides and non-stop book talk. She's tromped in the woods with me at night, circled Portland neighborhoods enough times to get the cops called on us (thankfully it never happened), and driven three hours just to see an island. You're the sister of my heart. Thanks for all you've done for me.

Last but not least, thanks to Valeri Miller for answering my questions about the Oregon justice system, and of course to my amazing editor Jessica Nollkamper. It's always a pleasure working with you!

ABOUT THE AUTHOR

Gemma James (a pseudonym for Christina Jean Michaels) loves to explore the darker side of sex in her fiction. She's morbidly curious about anything dark and edgy and enjoys exploring the deviant side of human nature. Her stories have been described as being "not for the faint of heart."

She lives with her husband and their four children—three rambunctious UFC/wrestling-loving boys and one girl who steals everyone's attention.

Find her online:

Blog - www.christinajmichaels.blogspot.com

Facebook - www.facebook.com/christinajmichaels